BRING ME THE HEAD OF QUENTIN TARANTINO

STORIES

Julián Herbert

Translated from the Spanish by
Christina MacSweeney

Graywolf Press

Originally published in 2017 as *Tráiganme la cabeza de Quentin Tarantino* by Penguin Random House Grupo Editorial, Mexico City.

The author would like to thank the Mexican Sistema Nacional de Creadores de Arte for its support.

This publication is made possible, in part, by the voters of Minnesota through a Minnesota State Arts Board Operating Support grant, thanks to a legislative appropriation from the arts and cultural heritage fund. Significant support has also been provided by Target Foundation, the McKnight Foundation, the Lannan Foundation, the Amazon Literary Partnership, and other generous contributions from foundations, corporations, and individuals. To these organizations and individuals we offer our heartfelt thanks.

Published by Graywolf Press
250 Third Avenue North, Suite 600
Minneapolis, Minnesota 55401

www.graywolfpress.org

Published in the United States of America

ISBN 978-1-64445-041-3

2 4 6 8 9 7 5 3 1
First Graywolf Printing, 2020

Library of Congress Control Number: 2019956748

Cover design: Walter Green

BRING ME THE HEAD OF QUENTIN TARANTINO

Also by Julián Herbert in English

Tomb Song

The House of the Pain of Others

Contents

The Ballad of Mother Teresa of Calcutta

For Armando J. Guerra and Javier Rodríguez Marcos

Stop kidding yourself: that thing you call "human experience" is just a massacre of onion layers. I use the word *massacre* in the generic sense, as any old interchangeable metaphor. Although, when you come to think of it, nothing tastes so much of blood as a dismembered onion, sliced on the glass surface of a table, smashed with a knife handle, or quartered with deep cuts. It must be the smell. The spray of clear liquid blinds the eyes of predators with tears and makes everything reek of vegetal flesh and hemorrhage, of hard, crystallized iron, blood flow, and vapor rather than solid matter. It's also true that when crushed, with its peeled, shorn stalk still attached, the onion looks less like a plant than a dead bug. So, yes: don't kid yourself, that thing you call "human experience" is just a massacre of onion layers. There's no getting away from it, particularly when it comes to telling a story. The first thing we do is choose the most perfect, most transparent, least damaged onion layer that happens to come our way.

That being the case, a few weeks ago I suggested to an old friend (after the signing of a contract and submission of an invoice on my part in exchange for the promise of a given sum of money) that his memoirs should open with the following anecdote:

Max took advantage of his rank in the French offices of Petróleos Mexicanos to fly from Paris to Montpellier. From there he took a cab to Sète to visit the tomb of Paul Valéry. It was the fall of 1981. Jorge Díaz Serrano had just stepped down as head of the state-owned company after cutting the price of oil. As part of the strategy of future presidential candidate Miguel de la Madrid to curb the extravagance of the soon-to-be-defunct government, the European headquarters had, for months, been pounded by the heavy artillery of auditors. Max, however, was not anxious; he merely found the situation irritating: the loss of his company car and driver was an annoyance. He'd spent the spring and summer commuting to and from work on the metro. Every weekday morning, he admired the gradual decomposition of the lacquered hairstyle of a chic, unwashed Parisian office worker. It was the image and scent of that putrefied hair spray that led him to open the safe containing the details of a government bank account to which he had exclusive discretional access. The balance was close to ten thousand dollars. Max assigned part of this sum to cover the expenses of his journey to Languedoc-Rousillon.

He was unmoved by the sight of Valéry's tomb, located on a secondary avenue of the necropolis and perched ignobly on a downward slope, very close to a standpipe with a leaky faucet. The coastal cemetery did, however, seem to him a perfect flawed gem, with its tombstones in the form of family albums, the roses made of glass, metal, or plaster in black granite vases, and the spectacular view of the Mediterranean. And then there was Sète: the market stinking of fisherman's ass; the Portuguese migrants, easily prostituted among the rocks on the shoreline; the bars where the only dish on the menu was also the house specialty: grilled clams and vin de pays de l'Hérault . . . All so pathetically picturesque that Max decided to make his stay indefinite.

That Wednesday, early in the afternoon, Basurto called.

"We're in the shit, Doc. They're taking us apart."

Maybe it was because that morning he'd had sex with a construction worker equipped with a laudable combination of menacing muscles and passive preferences, maybe because he'd ordered a kir royale with his lunchtime clams—something he rarely did; whatever the case, Max was feeling invulnerable.

"Tell them to go to hell."

"I've just handed the keys to your office to some middle-management type from the embassy," replied Basurto. "Good luck, Doc."

And then he hung up.

Max let the handset fall to one side of the desk. His best bet would be to check out of the hotel, buy a new suit and tie, and take a plane to Paris. Or Mexico, he thought. While he was visualizing these possibilities, he lay naked on the bed, groaning:

"Harrrupps, harrrupps."

(Max always says that a groan, uttered while lying completely naked on a rented bed, is like transcendental meditation.)

"Harrrupps."

There was a knock on the door.

"Qu'est-ce qui se passe là-bas, merde?"

Max sprang from the bed.

"Je vais bien, merci."

It took him a couple of hours and a great many costly international conference calls to get a full picture of the situation. Things were worse than he'd realized: not only had they sealed his office and frozen the official accounts at his disposal, but also they were discussing the possibility of declaring him a fugitive from justice. His immediate boss demanded that he present himself in Mexico City to respond to charges of an alleged megafraud involving overpricing in the acquisition of replacement parts. In addition, the auditors had found a cellar in Paris, registered in the name of PEMEX, full of assault weapons thought to be destined for the Nicaraguan government. Max hadn't even been aware of the existence of that cache.

He laughed silently: for five years he'd been the valet parking for delegates and government ministers who, without consulting him, were dreaming up and carrying out lucrative scams. Now he was going to have to take the rap, and his prosecutors would be the same individuals who were lining their pockets while handing him tips. Although he'd been in Europe for eight years, he decided that he'd never in fact left Mexico.

The next plane from Montpellier to Paris was scheduled for eleven that night. Max managed to get a seat on a connecting flight to Mexico City, departing from Charles de Gaulle at six in the morning. He could take a cab and spend three breakneck hours in his Parisian apartment. Perhaps. There was always the option of killing time in a bar, except that he wanted to stay sober until he showed up at the head office; he had a mild stomachache and it seemed stupid to go on abusing his digestive system twenty-four hours before the decisive battle. He could also cruise around Pigalle and find a prostitute, but he was in no mood to stick his dick into the amoeba-infested rectum of some obtuse, melodramatic migrant woman. To his way of thinking, the most irrational but also the most healthful choice would be to spend a solitary, sleepless night in the corridors of the airport.

I know the details of this story because I live under a curse: people like to tell me things and I can't stop them, because that's how I earn a living. I run a consultancy that specializes in evaluating and editing memories. Have you appreciated the juicy anecdotes told by some dull mayor at a patriotic dinner? Do you feel sympathy for the jaded singer bled dry by her handsome young husband? Are you moved by a book relating the hard work and personal tragedies of a telecommunications magnate? Do you by turns relish and feel horrified by the clever remarks and murders of some narco sicario who has been in prison for twenty years? Do the justifications of the stocky megalomaniac former president who left your country in ruins intrigue you? Then it's me you love: the majority of those revelations were designed in my office. I'm a personal memories coach, and that's why there isn't a blank page I wouldn't dare to get overfamiliar with. I'm the true author of the history of Mexico.

Everyone calls me El Negro. Yesterday I was a miracle worker, today I'm not even a shadow. I write anomalously, anonymously, by the piece. Every now and then I achieve some exceptional prose. I could have been one of the many fleeting new voices of Mexican literature, one of those kids who sell a handful of books over four or five years, only to become what they really are: glorified absurdities. I could have been one of them but I refused. Instead I studied business at Monterrey Tech. I refused because writers are a demented gang on overdrive who wouldn't be capable of finding a hat to shove up their own asses. I refused because I'm smart: I want to be corrupted by money, not flattery.

I discovered my talent (not for writing but for listening) in third grade. Miss Diana would occasionally ask me to stay back during recess to help her organize and check my classmates' homework. I was more than pleased to agree: she was a freckled redhead who smelled slightly of paella but also of lime juice, and wore tight-fitting white tops with wide necks, the sort I've always bought for my women. While she was putting ticks or crosses in notebooks with a bicolor pencil, she would tell me, all teary-eyed, about the dreadful things her boyfriend did to her. In a trembling, depraved voice (I know it was depraved because I was a child and she transmitted her narrative through unintelligible, moist murmurs), my teacher would detail those obscenities in terms that excluded the flesh. And that's why the images of torture and sexual abuse that came to my mind at the age of nine now appear in my adult fantasies as large-format, grainy close-ups showing people having sex with their clothes on.

Before the bell sounded, Miss Diana would dry her tears and pretend to regret her disclosures:

"I don't know why I tell you these things. You're too young to know what demons adults are," she'd say, stroking my hair and then asking hopefully, "When you grow up, you're never going to treat your girlfriend like that, are you?"

I'd say no, I never would. Then later, when I got home, I'd masturbate, evoking the catch in her husky voice until I finally felt a dull thump in my coccyx. Ejaculating before you can actually ejaculate is one of the most brutal experiences I know.

Was I ever really a child? I guess not. I've always been an ear: a fleshy seashell that oozes wax and strains everything it dreams through tiny teeth.

Max enters Charles de Gaulle with the bitterness of an exile, an aerial Aeneas choosing to pass through the Great Gate of Horn—the waters of the North Atlantic—en route to Hades, to the Federal District thereof. The year 1981 is the Paleozoic era of the duty-free zone, and it's midnight and all the shops and counters are closed. With nothing better to do than inspect the crevices of Paul Andreu's architectonic octopus, Max, whose luggage consists of only one bag, walks back and forth along the length of three of the terminal's four stories: like someone playing a three-dimensional game of hopscotch, he rides the Plexiglas snakes-and-ladders escalators that will become a classic pop image after the release of the Alan Parsons Project's second album, *I Robot*, a record the recently dismissed Mexican official will retain in his vinyl collection for over three decades but will never dare to play. He uses up two hours in that way. Lights are being switched off and the passenger areas are in shadow. He stops a couple of times in the restrooms, goes into a cubicle, and shits. Diarrhea. Nothing serious, just a twinge on the left side of his abdomen, and then a solitary lumpy stream of excrement deposited in one of the many heads and Cyclops eyes of the plumbing. Having had enough of traversing the airport's intestinal tunnels, he goes to his departure gate. It's still a long time until his plane leaves. He knows he'll be bored while pondering, amid all the metal and glass, the numbed solitariness of his buttocks against the hard seat. But there's nothing else on offer: airports are totalitarian states. He whiles away another hour looking out the windows at the blue and red lights on the runway. He has a French gay porno novel in his bag and a copy of *The Hydra Head* published by Argos: the only book by Carlos Fuentes he has liked enough to finish. But he doesn't feel like opening either of them. He's tired, wants to sleep. He's never been a great reader, even though he's spent five years doing a good job of pretending he is. Left-wing intellectualism is part of the uniform of Mexican bureaucracy. But books bore him. Movies are his thing. He's capable of watching five in a row without losing interest, memorizing the credits, the precision of the framing, the sensitive dialogue in *Deux hommes dans la ville* or *Les valseuses*, the unnatural intonation of *Rocco and His Brothers*, which has him hooked . . .

He'd arrived in Europe on a temporary visa. It was 1973, he was twenty-nine years old, and a bilateral agreement between the Mexican and Yugoslav governments had furnished him a scholarship to study film directing in Belgrade. He'd arranged his itinerary to include a week in Paris before the start of classes. During that time, his desire to become a socialist cineast was quenched by the vision of the city he'd dreamed of since childhood. The flight to Yugoslavia left without him. He went through a precarious period as a *clochard*, later doing any job that came his way: from a porter in a sex hotel to the ghostwriter of porno-exotic novels featuring Cecile & Gilles. Then José López Portillo's government opened a Parisian branch of PEMEX to administer the oil wealth and allow bureaucrats to charge their lavish vacations to the public purse. Thanks to a recommendation from a former boss, our frustrated filmmaker was employed as overseer of the caprices of power: a Ricardo Montalbán for the Fantasy Island of Mexican corruption.

(Max doesn't know it yet, but this will be the last time he'll set foot on French soil. He'll manage to avoid imprisonment and, after a few years, will regain the right to work in the public sector. His later life will be spent as the head of a provincial electoral body. However, the blue and red lights shining in the distance on the runway will be his final souvenir of Paris. That, and the predawn duel with Mother Teresa of Calcutta.)

(Every bottle of whisky has a tropical soul: once you've undressed it, you note that its ass is bigger and hotter than you thought. As I write this, I'm drinking the last shot from this bottle of Macallan and leafing through a pile of unpaid invoices. My business is going through a temporary crisis. I say "temporary" because I'm confident that this story will serve as a warning to my debtors.)

Sometime around four in the morning, a man appears at the departure gate. Max observes him: he's wearing jeans, a drill shirt, a beige jacket, and has a Nikon camera hanging around his neck. Not five minutes pass before another man, also armed with a camera, enters the waiting area and stands by the first. They joke together in French. It's obvious they haven't slept from the way they constantly knead their eyes. The one with the jacket is, in Max's opinion, good-looking: not too young, wiry, graying prematurely, and with manically intense blue eyes, Samuel Beckett eyes. Max tries to catch his attention but the guy ignores him. The next person to arrive is a member of the ground crew—cute, a little heavily made-up, wearing a small red hat, perhaps not very bright: the photographers make crude jokes about her, which she appears not to notice, or maybe she goes through life looking dumb as a protection against lust, the way *las brujeres* do on TV, thinks Max. A pale, thin, downy-cheeked priest joins them. After him comes an obese woman who introduces herself to the huddle as the public relations officer of something Max can't make out. Things are livening up in the departure lounge: another couple of photographers appear, three journalists holding Moleskines as if they were IDs, an elderly nun, two TV cameramen and their reporter with no equipment other than a scrawny butt, a big black man, impossible to miss because he's wearing a red-and-green outfit, and whose V for Victory torso is a delight to Max's eyes . . . For a moment the fugitive from PEMEX wonders if he himself might not be the focus of all this early morning paraphernalia. Maybe his situation has been made public and French journalists are about to bombard him with questions about his vile, corrupt behavior toward the Mexican nation, and a priest with the look of an ephebe wants to offer him solace by hearing his confession, and an obese public relations expert is here to plead his case to some judge or other, and some kind soul has sent a guardian angel in the shape of a muscular black body he could, cash down, drool over in the airport restrooms /

No. That's a ridiculous notion.

An unostentatious twin-engine passenger plane lands and taxies to the gate from which Max is due to depart. When the aircraft comes to a halt and the engines have been shut off, Max notices a stir among the media and lay public at the other end of the lounge. The passengers descend a short set of steps at the door of the Fokker F27—after a decade of regular flights, Max has become an expert in the models. The aircraft is almost empty: only seven shadowy figures emerge from it. They walk along an imaginary corridor marked on the tarmac with fluorescent paint to a glass access door, where the cute-but-dumb member of the ground crew awaits them with a smile.

Max's stomach contracts, forcing a spicy pocket of greasy air upward to his gullet. Who is that elderly dyke with skin like parchment, a boxer's nose, cracked lips, and a perfect smile, that bent but definitely not frail passenger who looks just like the Disney witch in *Snow White*? She's third in the single file of travelers. Her head is covered by a white cloth with blue stripes. He knows her. She's someone famous. It's almost a minute before he recognizes her as that repulsive nun Teresa of Calcutta. The reason for Max's revulsion isn't her good-heartedness but that sense of nausea caused by being in the proximity of pest controllers: people who spend too much time in the company of toxic, purulent, snuffling creatures. There's no way you can speak calmly about the contact those people have with Evil. There has to be something infectious in the lymph nodes of their souls.

But he also knows that he's seduced: he's never been able to pass up the opportunity to get close to a celebrity. So far, he's had his photo taken with Celia Cruz and Irma Serrano, José Luis Cuevas, Archbishop Miguel Darío Miranda y Gómez, Carlos López Moctezuma, and Carlos Monsiváis. In years to come he'll have better luck, and will pose with Silvia Pinal, Ninel Conde, Angélica María, and Franco

Nero, among others. But on that day in Charles de Gaulle airport, with Max's mouth reeking of semidigested seafood and his guts gurgling with an excess of gas, the aberrant Mother Teresa of Calcutta is the highest card in his deck. Max gets to his feet and, screwing up his courage, swallowing his bitter reflux, makes his way unsmilingly toward the welcome committee with his right hand outstretched, just as any other atrophied amiable zombie would do on encountering the philanthropic face of absolute evil.

There's a sense of epiphany in the moment. It must have something to do with the vigor with which Max approaches the nun: he floats on a cloud of beatitude with a rigid forearm by way of a calling card, as if he were the Angel of the Lord about to impregnate a geriatric crone. The media and lay public move aside to let him pass. Perhaps some of them think he's a friend and patron, or an eminent ecclesiastic of uncertain identity. Some of the photographers get to work, calculating light levels and the framing of their images. Mother Teresa herself is struck by the lightning bolt of Faith and shifts her gaze from the group to Max, still a few yards away. She slowly extends her right hand and smiles, causing a surge of wrinkles to sweep across her face: her expression, intended to be sweet, is toxic. Max takes two more strides before realizing what is about to occur. Mother Teresa's smile is a bottomless pit: behind it is an old person with swollen yellow feet covered in flies, and a dark-skinned man using the butt of his rifle to anally rape a girl, and a group of laughing children with rotten teeth, and six teenagers displaying their sex to passersby in Sonagachi, and a fund-raising gala where the downy-cheeked priest is sucking the dick of the black guy in the toilets, and a dozen skeletal women selling wilted green vegetables in the Calcutta traffic, and the sewage in which a group of partying adolescents dance barefoot, and people collecting human shit with their hands, and an orchard where women and children kneel among blossom-laden trees, waiting to receive a bullet in the back of the head, and the explosion in a power plant justified by a Naxalite-Maoist commando, Japanese bombers attacking a port and /

Max's stomach becomes his mind and memory when, in reaction to the smiling abyss of Mother Teresa's face, he gives a preliminary belch and then feels something unstoppable rising up his throat: a thick stream of puke composed of partially digested clams and wine that falls onto the extended hand and spotless headdress of the damned old witch crammed to the brim with lepers. Mother Teresa is frozen to the spot. With horror and apprehension, Max calculates that his next emission of vomit will reach the woman's face. The bystanders intervene: some to hustle the Holy Woman aside, others to remove Max.

"What's *wrong* with you?" a stern voice demands.

Max raises his eyes and recognizes the Samuel Beckett photographer. He wants to explain, but all that comes out of his mouth is another dark, viscous stream that falls at the feet of Samuel, who, annoyed and slightly fearful—Max suddenly recalls that since *The Exorcist*, vomit is seen by the lay public as proof of the presence of Lucifer—turns and puts distance between himself and the puke.

The airport congregation has withdrawn to the far end of the lounge, its back turned to him, protecting Mother Teresa with its body; it turns its shit(ty) scared head to Max in pure Linda Blair mode. Max discovers that the only way he can live down the humiliation is by fulfilling the expectations of this bunch of superstitious believers. He tries to catch Mother Teresa's eye again, gives a pantomime devil laugh, and walks off (the whites of his eyes showing, his body wracked by epileptic contortions) in search of a restroom. He vomits three times into the bowl, cleans his teeth with a folding toothbrush and a thin line of paste, shits runny feces for a quarter of an hour, and then returns to the profaned waiting area, imagining how he will tell the story of what has just happened: how Satan briefly possessed him and how the Evil Enemy was vanquished by the pious gaze of Mother Teresa.

But the lounge is empty. The floor clean.

Max sits down again. He feels satisfied, freed from the heaviness of indigestion. A few minutes go by. A family arrives: father, mother, two not-bad-looking fair-haired boys. It's obvious they haven't slept from the way they constantly knead their eyes. A cute member of the airline ground crew goes to the counter by the departure gate. Another group of travelers turns up and disperses among the rows of seats. Max prepares himself for the flight to the Federal District of Hell.

—

That's not how it happened. What Max told me was that once, early in the morning, in the airport of some European city, he found himself in the company of a group of nuns. Although they were unaccompanied, with no security staff or media in tow, Max is certain that one of them was Mother Teresa of Calcutta.

"So what did you do?"

"Nothing," he answered. Then he thought for a moment and added, "I hid my watch. I was afraid they'd try to steal it to feed the frigging poor."

Apologies if I'm ruining the story for you. I'm doing it to take my revenge on Max and also, maybe, to give myself the pleasure of depositing a little vomit on those readers who adore straightforward literature, with no digressions or contradictions or shortcuts, those adult babies who read as if the story were the nipple of a baby bottle. Being an autobiography and personal memories coach isn't easy. Not only do you have to find the right technique for converting a string of trivialities into a pearl necklace of adventures, also you have to grit your teeth as you write and have a strong stomach. The stomach of a whore. And, above all, you have to learn how to collect. Most people have a problem paying for a better version of themselves. They come sniveling to you with their grammatically moronic A4 sheets and their long-drawn-out, stuttering stories. But just as soon as you've initiated them into the art of converting their heap of crap into an elegant speech or a judicious memoir, they begin to look at you with derision in their eyes: those poor wretches assume they were the real authors of their recollections. I can deal with that. What I won't tolerate is the lack of remuneration. That's why I rolled out this experimental payment strategy: hijacking the memories and anecdotes of certain clients and offering them as short stories—in exchange for a modest sum—to cultural publications and literary supplements.

It's not my intention to betray anyone. I apologize if I have. I'd never have been indiscreet enough to publish this story if Max had paid up on time. But he didn't. If I've chosen him, my old friend, as an example of this mode of blackmail, it's to demonstrate to the clients that I'm not willing to make concessions. I'm a true Mexican businessman, and that means I'm trained to carry out or condone any low-down action in exchange for money. Don't fool yourself: that thing you call "human experience" is just a massacre of onion layers.

M. L. Estefanía

I was forty years old and smoking between twenty and thirty rocks a week when I transformed myself into Marcial Lafuente Estefanía. At 120 a Ziploc plus the small change you leave for a can of soda each time you score, do the math. Not even the most corrupt tabloid journalist in the state capital could have kept up a lifestyle like that. And I know because I was that journalist. I'd start as soon as my shift at the newspaper was over, accompanied by some newbie from the prosecutor's office or one of the off-duty patrolmen who are sometimes given free samples of the goods on the market. Any one of those people would have had the guts to stop before the sun came up. Not me; I was off my head 24-7. One good toke lasts five or ten minutes. If you want to keep on an even keel, you have to suck on the aluminum like a baby bottle, clean the perforations regularly with a needle, and have a Marlboro perpetually lit: the crackhead's skill lies as much in the rhythm of the inhalation as in the precise application of ash. All this intoxicating paraphernalia made it almost impossible for me to put in a full day's work. When I was fired, I telephoned my compadre Esquivel for help.

"What can you do?" he asked.

Esquivel is the mayor of a border municipality, and the centenary of the Revolution was coming up. I offered him a lecture on the strategic role of rebel customs officers in financing the Constitutionalist Army after the Ten Tragic Days of 1913.

He roared with laughter.

"You think my wannabe Texan ranchies give a shit about the Revolution? You'd be better off talking to them about Zane Grey. And what's the problem with your old line of work?"

There was no question of going back to that.

"La Gente might get the planks out."

I asked for a couple of days to come up with another topic, then called again.

"I can do something on popular culture: a talk about Marcial Lafuente Estefanía. They all know his books there on the border, and many of the plots are based on Spanish Golden Age plays."

Esquivel, who had experience in showbiz, put it another way:

"Hey, we'll tell a little white lie: from now on, you're Marcial. You'll come onstage with a holster and my Remington. You'll be dressed as a cowboy. I'll take care of that: I've got a Boss of the Plains here somewhere, we can see if it fits you. I'll pay five thousand pesos plus expenses for the first talk, and then, if things work out, we'll sell the idea of a tour to the Public Education people: I've got a contact there."

I hated the thought of pirating the author of over three thousand Western novels. And what if someone filed a lawsuit? But my craving was so strong that I agreed, not before first begging Esquivel to deposit an advance in my bank account that same afternoon.

The first event, held less than a mile from the Río Bravo in a dirt lot with a concrete stage, was very well attended. There isn't a god-fearing soul east of the Mapimí Basin and west of Laredo who hasn't read at least one pocket book by the author of *Terror in Cheyenne*. Our success was partly due to the publicity material my wonderful mayor produced: posters with aqua and fuchsia text on a black background, like the ones they use to promote *grupero* bands. But I excelled myself too. I recited from memory the best passages of *The Colt's Caress*, strode back and forth across the stage brandishing the microphone like a revolver, adapted Clint Russell's dialogues from *Duty First*, and told stories filched from the repertoire of the legendary Saltillo Chronicler . . . I was given a standing ovation. After the event I signed a mountain of books published by Brainsco, most of them with broken spines and pages missing, and more than one with disgusting stains. By the end, I was in a cold sweat: withdrawal was killing me. As a version of honor among thieves, I'd told Esquivel about my addiction and he'd sent an official car to take me to a small restaurant on the Ribereña highway, not very far from Ciudad Acuña, where we were to meet. While paying for the gear, sorting out the can, lighting the ash, inhaling, watching a Mexican Navy helicopter maneuvering overhead, and waiting for the smoke to reach my lungs, I made a mental summary of the ways my homeland had changed: since the start of the war on drugs, it had become easier and more lucrative to set up a cocaine outlet than an OXXO store.

If only that thought had never crossed my mind.

My compadre Esquivel was a politician who knew how to swim in dirty water. He'd started off as a leader of the youth wing of the PRI and used that position to blackmail the Confederación Nacional Campesina into appointing him head of the communal land commission for Fraustro, an important rail freight junction. He gained the post without ever having set foot on a farm. Small-time theft had been a local tradition in Fraustro for decades: the inhabitants bribed the brakemen and drivers to "lose" one or two of the washing machines being transported from the nearby CINSA plant. Esquivel revolutionized this custom by teaming up with a councilman from the municipality of General Cepeda to ambush at least one train a week and remove the entire cargo. When the Federal Police decided to get involved in the affair, my friend abandoned a small truck bearing the municipal logo and loaded with stolen white goods by the tracks and went on the run.

While he was living on the margins of the law, Esquivel diversified: he bribed his way into obtaining a concession for cab services, created a music marketing agency in association with Servando Cano and his gunrunning brother Choto, coordinated electoral campaigns behind the scenes . . . Around ten years later, when the stormy seas of his period as a commissioner and fugitive had calmed, he put his name forward to run for office in his hometown's municipal elections. The PRI said no. When representatives of PAN and PRD heard of this snub, they formed an alliance to offer him the candidacy. By accepting their offer, Esquivel was killing two birds with one stone: not a single political activist found it convenient to refer to his dark past. He swept the opposition off the map.

A certain Camargo, who drove one of the cabs in a fleet owned by Esquivel, used to supply a schoolmistress named Bonilla—an important figure in the education union of the northeast—with marijuana and cocaine. The driver and union leader eventually became quite close. It was Camargo who introduced us to her. Bonilla took an interest in our project, and by calling in a few favors she succeeded in getting the Secretariat of Public Education to offer us a contract through one of its reading programs: a hundred talks by M. L. Estefanía in rural schools and community colleges. The total budget was 1,360,000 pesos, of which 250k would come to me, 500k clear of tax to Bonilla, and the remainder, less expenses, to Esquivel.

"Don't give it a second thought," he replied when the withdrawal symptoms had me so low that I expressed my qualms. "It's not fraud: we're working in the gray zone created by postmodern education and culture. The death of the author and all that crap you go on about in your talks."

"And the kickback to Bonilla?"

"It's not a kickback. Just an age-old tradition."

Esquivel requested a temporary leave of absence from the council: he was going to protect his investment by accompanying me throughout the tour.

Two hundred and fifty thousand pesos for three months' work

is not an inconsiderable sum, especially when you take into account that my workday would be under two hours, but money goes up in smoke when you're a rodeo star. Esquivel's thing was lap dancers: he was capable of spending whole days going to the back room with one girl after another. I'd accompany him to the clubs because you could always get a line there, if not something better. Between us, the mayor and I covered the expenses of Camargo, who, on Bonilla's instruction, had joined the expedition as bodyguard and driver. He was very tall, well built, and about ten years younger than us, but his beer gut and premature baldness made him look older.

Our respective vices were anything but scarce. There was never any problem finding a brothel with the lights on late at night or a corner with a teenager carrying a black backpack, sometimes still in school uniform, selling snow and rock. It was not uncommon for a supplier, at the sight of my offstage attire, which included items by Dockers and Girbaud, to ask in a slightly somber tone:

"You're the gunslinger who gave the talk this morning, right?"

I'd nod, open my Levi's jacket, and give him a brief glimpse of Esquivel's ancient Remington 1875 Army Outlaw single-action revolver, which, from sheer paranoia, I always carried at my waist, loaded with old lead-alloy bullets and black powder bought from an antiques dealer in Monclova. After that gesture the adolescents would supply me with the bulkiest rocks in their stash.

In Sierra Mojada, where—despite the fact that it had once hosted a performance by the soprano Ángela Peralta—it's impossible to find a cab, I followed the instructions of a senile miner: "Just go along the rails to La Esmeralda and you'll find my grandson there with his stuff." In San Pedro, a country-style goth girl escorted me free of charge to the corner where the dealers hang out, on a street named after a poet, only two blocks from city hall. In Boquillas del Carmen—a town in the Sierra, across the border from Big Bend National Park, and accessible only by light aircraft—every kid for miles around came to greet us on arrival.

"It's just that they rarely catch sight of the plane," apologized the head of the rural school. "They only ever hear it landing with its cargo at night."

In Viesca, I had an encounter that turned out to be providential. I was coming out of the Cultural Center after one of my talks (still wearing my gunman outfit) when a Ford Lobo with tinted glass braked suddenly beside me. The driver opened the window. He was in his early thirties, blond, dressed in black, and wearing shades.

"What's up, Prof?"

I recognized him immediately: about ten years before, he'd been one of my journalism students in a graphic design college that was finally closed down for being unaccredited. I recalled his features but not his name.

"Just earning a buck. I'm on a lecture tour."

"Dressed as a rodeo clown?"

He was trying to get my hackles up, but something in the shining block of darkness behind his sunglasses gave me the feeling that the unruly, mule-headed kid I'd known all those years ago had turned into a sleekly terrifying animal.

"That's what they asked for . . . ," I replied in justification.

He smiled.

"I get it. Good luck, Prof."

He closed the window and pulled away, burning rubber.

The really big drain on Esquivel's finances was the presence of Violeta Vallardes—Camargo and I renamed her Violeta the Violent—a Nicaraguan stripper based in Sabinas who had joined us halfway through the trip. She looked just like a chubbier version of the porn star Lucía Lapiedra. One evening when we were alone at a restaurant table (Esquivel had gone to the restroom), I said:

"You look just like Lucía Lapiedra."

She glared at me and spit into my glass.

"Forget it: that dumb broad'd suck me off if I so much as looked at her."

She must have found out from the TV or the internet in Cuatro Ciénagas that, after hooking up with a sports commentator, Lucía

Lapiedra had quit her porn career, gotten married, won a reality show, and turned herself into the tenderhearted and popular Miriam Sánchez Cámara. That really did turn Violeta on: she invited me for a moonlight swim in Los Mezquites and offered up what she'd initially refused.

We lived in a paradise of open-air stages, broken microphones, outdated costumes, and amazing landscapes. But then the money ran out. Esquivel must have realized what was coming better than any of us, because during a pause in the tour (we were staying in a trailer park motel near Sacramento), he came to my room and threw a folder crammed with photocopies onto the bed.

"I've got an idea for making more cash," he said. "All we need is a well-designed plan and your baritone voice."

"What's all that stuff?"

"Data. Telephone numbers, bank statements, home addresses. All women's."

"So?"

"So I've done my part. Now it's up to you to cold-call and threaten them. You tell them we're an armed commando group and we're just around the corner from the house. And we're gonna kill them unless they hand over a given sum of money."

Without giving me even a moment to protest, Esquivel dropped a packet of crack the size of a guava next to the folder.

"Consider this an engagement ring," he said with a smile before walking out of the room.

—

It's not as easy as it might seem. The important thing (I didn't learn this from any criminal but from my nephew who works in telemarketing) is to have a detailed script. Scenarios: "If the prospective client says *x*, apply interaction three. If the prospective client responds *y*, follow the steps laid out in interaction seven down to the last word."

"Good afternoon, señora."

It's almost always women who answer.

"This is Comandante Marcial Lafuente Estefanía of the Federal Police. We're following up on a report made from this telephone number."

The aim is to prevent the woman from cutting off the call by any available means.

At first we worked catch-as-catch-can: making calls on the road between performances of our Western show, holed up in the restrooms of gas stations, in motel rooms with the television on mute . . . As the business began to grow, we thought it would be a good idea to set up an office. Esquivel got hold of a dilapidated shack in the communal village of La Pócima, halfway between Cuatro Ciénagas and San Pedro de las Colonias. We moved in as soon as the tour finished.

"Are you sure you didn't make that call, señora? The communications people say we have a woman's voice on tape."

Most Mexicans are genetically incapable of distinguishing between a criminal and a policeman, which is why this interrogation method is so effective. Thinking aloud, trying to come up with an answer, the prospective client gives essential information that, a few minutes later, will allow her to be blackmailed: the number of people living in the house, their ages, when they come and go, any people who are employed in the house . . . On good days, with a talkative prospective client, you can even learn the color of the house, the children's first names, and the make of the family car.

There was no electricity in La Pócima. After dark we had just two oil lamps. By day, the landscape bordering the highway is like jeweled folds: green and blue mountains, white dunes, mounds of exposed virgin rock that made you think of giant hands emerging from the land of the dead to punch the sun. At night, that beauty is put on pause: it's all just black cold and a wind that tastes of road metal.

The shack was built of unfinished cement blocks, had a corrugated cardboard roof and joints reinforced with railroad ties stolen from the Ferrocarriles Nacionales de México by the former owner of the property. It was a basic one-story building, set at an angle to the highway, with a door of cracked wood and a window that was in fact a huge hole looking out onto the white, gritty flatlands. To gain a little privacy, we hung a sheet over the hole and piled up the boxes of inactive files Esquivel brought from his city hall office to create the illusion of a two-room house. Beyond this division, in what could be called the bedroom, were a couple of folding cots, where we slept in shifts. Under the window was an orange futon belonging to Violeta that could be used only with her authorization. Beside the futon we installed a large trestle table, piled with directories, notebooks, and disposable cell phones. Finally, positioned precisely parallel to the doorway, as if standing guard, was Esquivel's old, heavy metal writing desk.

We never returned the Suburban that Bonilla lent us for the tour. Camargo had a DVD player in there on which we watched old urban Westerns starring the Almada brothers, *Deadly Enemies*, or Champions League games that a barman in San Pedro recorded for us. Sometimes we'd venture out at night to the strip clubs in Torreón; they were almost always empty. The city had been under siege since the government gave the *plaza* to Los Señores, sparking a war with the cartel controlling Durango. The Nazas River had become a frontier drawn with blood. Gunfire could be heard night and day to the west of Avenida Colón. The area around the Alianza Market, once the heart of the most sordid joys, was a ghost town. Urban legend had it that any kid who dared to cross the river to buy drugs in Gómez or Lerdo would be a corpse by sunrise.

"We're absolutely certain that the call was made on your telephone. My boys lost two pickups and one of them has been arrested. So tell me, where do we go from here?"

You have to reveal yourself at just the right moment, when the prospective client seems most confused. The best way is to use a mix of drama and restraint without lowering the bar to violence.

"Do you know what the last letter of the alphabet is, lady? Well, that's us. Our men are just around the corner from your house, awaiting instructions."

Esquivel ordered us to carry handguns. He bought a Smith & Wesson 686 Nickel with a dark wood grip for himself. Violeta got a really useless kitschy pink Lorcin. Camargo carried a well-worn .38 Super that had acquired a gray patina from all the grease. I was offered a Beretta Cougar, but refused it. I preferred to hang on to my old Remington.

Although we sometimes changed roles, the functions of each member of the group were well-defined. Esquivel was always in charge of logistics, administration, and the agenda; he was the brains behind the operation. Camargo's remit was transportation, purchases, and security, plus he brought the list of potential clients that Bonilla obtained from some obscure private-education coordinating body associated with the SPE. I was the public face (or rather voice) of the business: the sales representative. Violeta the Violent's mission was one for which her conventional beauty proved most useful: debt collection. We received the payments via money orders deposited in branches of Western Union or Banco Azteca. While I was working the client from a disposable cell phone, Esquivel would be on another telephone coordinating our girlfriend's movements.

We'd begun to openly share Violeta's affections toward the end of the tour. To my surprise, and that of Esquivel (he'd already had his suspicions that something was going on between Violeta and me and had thrown that accusation in my face during a euphoric stopover in the Hotel Rincón del Montero), she was also with Camargo. Esquivel didn't find the situation funny in any sense, but neither did he take it to heart. We came to an agreement that Camargo and I would contribute a percentage of what he'd paid Los Lenones, the sex-trafficking cartel that had sold her in Sabinas, and after that we split the profits of our savage telemarketing operation four ways. Camargo proposed that we seal the deal with a group sex session. He ended up with Violeta and I got Esquivel. We never again mentioned or repeated the affair.

"Don't even think about showing your face, you scumbag, or you're screwed. I'm watching you from here: one more wrong move and I'll shoot out the fucking windows."

The delicate part of the procedure is managing the hysteria. I consider myself a master of that particular art. There's a moment when you have to start shouting at them, using the dirtiest words in your repertoire, making them feel that their lives mean nothing to you. That part isn't complicated. The tricky thing is to convince them, from a distance of five hundred miles, that you're at the door of their home, watching them. The majority cut the call at the first sign of a raised voice. You have to make fifteen or twenty calls before someone takes the bait. But one hit's enough: when panic sets in, you can squeeze the very last cent out of them. It's just a matter of keeping them on the line during the long-drawn-out bank transactions. Those can take hours. The failed calls, on the other hand, waste five or ten minutes of your time.

To keep myself alert and aggressive, I'd alternate telephone numbers with crack bombs. At first the urge for the next smoke was so overwhelming that on a couple of occasions I came close to losing a sale that had already gone through. Once, when I had a man inside his car in the middle of traffic, on his way to the bank, I said:

"Don't speed up, you bastard. I'm watching you."

"But I'm stopped at a red light."

I hung up.

With practice I learned how to play my cards. To smoke the soda between interventions without the sound of my inhalations sneaking through the microphone. To use the hands-free headset like an invisible video game screen. In that way, I could, on average, close two forty-thousand-peso deals between eight in the morning and four in the afternoon: over a million and a half a month. In the business, that made me the fastest cell phone in the West. Don't judge me: it's the same scam convicts used to pull, offering nonexistent prizes in exchange for phone cards so they could talk to their families for free. I didn't vote for the change. I just altered the script, adapted it for the country you chose.

A shame that things weren't always so sweet. At night, after sleeping a couple of hours to recover from the crack tremors, I'd feel like any old rapist who messes with women because he's afraid to try it with men. If it was my turn, and we were both in the mood, I'd have sex with Violeta in the open air or inside the Suburban. I always tried to do it gently, with all the tenderness I was capable of, thinking only of her comfort and pleasure. It was my way of asking forgiveness of the women I'd abused during working hours. My job gave me the same sensation I got from smoking rock: something close to ecstasy when I was holding in the smoke, but absolute horror the moment I exhaled. My colleagues used to make fun of me because I'd wake in the early morning crying after a nightmare in which I'd tortured my deceased mother, putting the black barrel of my gun in her mouth.

—

I'm forbidden from writing their name. We call them Los Señores or La Compañía, La Gente, Los Patrones. They are (east of the Mapimí Basin and west of Laredo) the law for those who follow the path of lawlessness.

Camargo had warned us from the start:

"You can't go doing whatever you please. You have to give advance notice and ask for their blessing."

We didn't listen. I frivolously decided that it wasn't part of my job description: that it was Esquivel's territory. He opted for discretion and exemption: he'd gone back to fulfilling his mayoral functions (at least in theory) and was on good terms with both the state and federal governments. We were told that the details of the tour were not to be revealed under any circumstances. But a Suburban parked alongside a desert highway and DVD recordings of all the Champions League games made by a small-town barman aren't things that can be easily hidden. So they found us.

They didn't even take the trouble to turn up at night. It must have been around four in the afternoon. The beginning of November. The sun was beating down but a wind stirred the air. Esquivel was napping with his feet up on the desk and the Boss of the Plains tipped over his face. Violeta was lying on her futon reading a magazine. I'd taken a break between calls to smoke my bomb, sitting on the cot behind the inactive-archive wall. Camargo was outside, scanning the highway in both directions through binoculars.

He came into the shack, holding down his baseball cap with his left hand. Something was clearly worrying him.

"They're coming, Doc. It's a metallic blue Pathfinder, stopped at the roadside. Tinted glass. The roof's covered in GPS gear."

Violeta and I rose from our respective beds.

"Relax," drawled Esquivel in a drowsy voice. "It's probably nothing."

"Probably," replied Camargo. "But you don't see wheels like that around here."

"Probably just passing through, if it is them."

"Probably, but this isn't their territory. There's an army roadblock in Ciénagas."

Esquivel took his Smith & Wesson 686 from a drawer and laid it on the desk under some papers. Camargo released the safety of his pistol and positioned himself opposite the door with his right hand behind his back. Violeta put the Lorcin down the front of her dress. Without any real conviction, I followed their example, fetched the Remington from the trestle table, and put it on my bed.

"How much cash have you all got on you?" asked Esquivel.

"About six thou," I answered: I always tried to have more than enough in my billfold to buy crack in rural watering holes. Violeta and Camargo didn't reply.

We waited.

I chain-smoked two bombs. Then, finally, we heard the vehicle: an engine gradually slowing down.

"I'll take them out," said Camargo to no one in particular and headed for the door.

"No way," ordered Esquivel. "We'll negotiate."

The engine hadn't even died when a bullet came through the door and hit Camargo in the right shoulder, knocking him back and spinning him around.

"Drop it, you bastard," shouted a voice from beyond the door. "Drop the weapons."

Violeta and Esquivel didn't move a muscle. I threw the Remington under the cot and curled up on the floor. From there I was able to see what happened next through a crack between two boxes.

A fair-skinned man with a shaved head, wearing a black T-shirt and jeans, came through the door. I recognized him immediately: it was the former student I'd come across in Viesca. What was his name?

"Drop it," repeated my student to Camargo. He was very calm.

Camargo obeyed. He knelt on the concrete floor and raised his uninjured arm above his head. My former student picked up the .38 Super and put it in his belt. He walked toward Esquivel, while, behind him, another two men in black tees and dark blue jeans stood on either side of the door, one outside and the other inside the shack. The man outside, who had a cadaveric appearance and a straggly mustache, was carrying a pistol. The other—older, with sparse graying hair—had a Kalashnikov.

"You the mayor?" asked my former student.

"Yes, boss. Mayor Esquivel, at your service."

Esquivel made to stand but was commanded to stay where he was with a casual movement of my former student's hand.

"Where's your rodeo clown?"

"Pardon?"

"Prof," he (what was his name?) shouted. "Come on out, Prof."

"Would you like a shot of brandy?" offered Esquivel, making another attempt to stand. "Just to help the negotiations along."

"I don't negotiate with ghosts."

The pale-skinned guy fired two bullets. Both hit Esquivel in the face and he fell to the ground, grasping a few sheets of paper. The Smith & Wesson lay uncovered on the desk.

Violeta took the Lorcin from her cleavage. Camargo gave a cry and, passing with exasperating slowness between the two guys guarding the door, fled painfully toward the scrub. Violeta managed to let off two shots: one hit an oil lamp and the other went into the wall. Then the Lorcin jammed. My former student loomed over my lover, grabbed her throat, and deftly pushed her back against the boxes. He smashed the barrel of his gun into her face and, with the other hand, punched her in the stomach. The boxes moved. For a moment his eyes crossed with mine through the crack in the inactive-archive wall.

I straightened out and slid to my right until I found another chink in the archive wall. Through the window, I could see Camargo running toward a distant mountain. He was stumbling across the loose white earth. By looking through the crack at a different angle, I could see what was happening to my left. I watched the cadaveric gunman standing by the doorjamb take aim at Camargo and fire three times. I turned my eyes to the window and witnessed Camargo gradually decelerate until he fell flat on his face. He was clearly dead.

My former student threw Violeta onto the orange futon and turned his back. Looking at the man with the AK-47, he nodded in her direction. His subordinate took two steps forward and emptied the ammo in his assault rifle—thirty cartridges—into her. The air was filled with the shards and smell of shattered concrete. My former student jumped behind the metal desk (which, until that afternoon, had belonged to Esquivel) to protect himself from the flying fragments.

"With your pistol, moron," he screamed.

But the gunfire had lasted scarcely a few seconds.

Silence reigned for a moment.

Outside, the sun was still beating down.

"Come out, Prof," said the weary voice of my former student (what was his name?). "It's El Checo. I'm not going to kill you."

I dragged myself from behind the inactive-archive wall and, crying all the while, embraced his knees.

"Don't kill me, Chequito. Be merciful. I swear it wasn't my fault. They told me everything had been arranged."

The burning metal on my neck made me shy back but I didn't let go of his legs.

"That's how I like it, you bastard, a show of respect. I only came for the mayor. You three were just going to get the plank."

After a pause, he added:

"That bitch had more balls than you."

He ordered his men to load Violeta's and Camargo's bodies into the Suburban. Then he explained to one of them how to dispose of the goods. The man headed into the sunset at the wheel of what had been our car. Checo and the other gunman made a space in the Pathfinder for Esquivel's body and for me. We drove east for a while. It was beginning to get dark. A couple of miles before Cuatro Ciénagas, we turned off the highway into the limestone dunes. They motioned for me to get out.

"Right then, baby," said Checo, putting on a pair of gloves. "I'm gonna switch things up and teach you something for a change."

He beat me with a thick plank. First on the buttocks and the back. When I tried to get up to run, he beat my shoulders and head until I was half-dead.

I spent the rest of the night on the dunes. The cold woke me. I managed to get on my feet and hobble to town. It was already midmorning by the time I arrived in the square. I went to Doc's restaurant and begged the waiter to let me use the restroom to wash off the blood. The little fucker took pity on me.

I waited two days before returning to Saltillo on borrowed money and a begged ride. There, I discovered that Esquivel's body had ended up in Monclova: they'd hung him from one of the thousand new bridges constructed by the state government. There was a sign on his chest saying, "This is what happens to people who don't ask first." Or at least that's what a former colleague at the newspaper told me: the local press and television stations didn't say a word about the affair. The national media talked about the killing of a valiant border-town mayor by an organized-crime gang. I never found out what happened to the remains of Violeta and Camargo. An attempt was made on Bonilla's life and since then the Feds have given her a bodyguard.

I stopped doing rock for one or two weeks. Then I went back on it:

there's no hope for me now. I'm living with Karen, a toothless junkie twenty years my junior. We make a living from a new version of an old scam: drugging people in supermarket parking lots and taking their billfolds. We approach them on any pretext at all (she almost always does that part) and smear belladonna on their skin. It's a dangerous drug. To avoid poisoning ourselves, we have to cover our fingertips in wax before touching the stuff. It takes a few minutes for the effects to show: the client experiences disorientation, blurred vision, partial paralysis, dizziness . . . Sounds classy, right? Good old Medici intrigue. The reality is we're birds of prey. We earn a pittance, but at least there are no plankings here.

Proud? Of course I'm not proud. I'm writing this anonymously from an unnamed location and I'm going to send it to a friend with a request to publish it as a sort of confession: I'm not Marcial Lafuente Estefanía, just the coward of the county. Don't despise me or hate me. After all, what I am is the embodiment of that miracle you pray for every night: an outlaw who's decided to throw down his gun.

White Paper

For Carlos Amorales

1

They brought us here with the promise that we'd get some hands-on experience. Our specialty is crime scene analysis. This particular scene has become a labyrinth. The house had been purified. Instead of the usual red spatter patterns there are white stains on all the walls. A pale powder covers the furniture and the fixtures in the bathroom and kitchen. It's as if a whole family had been massacred in a tub of whitewash. We don't know who we are, what authority we have to be here, or when our task will be completed. We don't even know one another. Our only credential is a vaguely scientific attitude as we take detailed photographs of a corner of a room or gather evidence in a bedroom and our shoulders happen to touch; nothing else unites us. In contrast to the flush of dawn on the outer edges of the investigation, our identities are obscure. And what's more, we're hemmed in by music that prevents us from going outdoors, even to the garden. To figure out where the music is coming from, and so to hide from it, we have to peek through the lace curtains. Some of us doubt that those things covering the windows are really lace curtains. They say that the curtains are evidence: one more white spatter pattern that bleeds into everything. Others think we are ghosts: murder victims eternally trapped in the private residence of our extinction. Yet others doubt if it's that simple: it would be easier if we were just ghosts rather than witnesses for the prosecution. That way we wouldn't have to sleep in a huddle on the floor each night or perform juggling tricks to safeguard the disgusting evidence on the walls. We wouldn't have to suffer hunger, thirst, or drowsiness. We wouldn't sweat or smell so bad. We wouldn't have to degrade our evenings filling in form after form in minute writing. The one indication that we might be dead is our recognition that we are on the verge of insanity: madness is the nearest thing to being a ghost.

2

The music hates us. It reinvents itself every day. It's fast and it throbs in the trees. We have no idea how big the garden is, which is why we don't dare venture across it: what if the music were to catch up with us and slice us in two before we reached the street? If it was at least monotonous, we'd have gotten the better of it by now. But it isn't. At times it sounds like a military drum or a tabla flooding bedrooms and bathrooms with its needles of fine rain. At other times it's exactly like the scratching of a fountain pen amplified five hundredfold, a stylus generating notes as it draws the grooves of our brains on scraps of paper. On yet other occasions it is a string of keys hanging menacingly from the branches. A small forest of lynched pianos. If it was possible to hear just one of those pianos at a time, we'd be able to enjoy it, even knowing that it was a corpse. But hearing them in unison is like sinking into quicksand made of air.

3

Someone is contaminating the evidence. There's no other explanation. We've spent too long (it could be hours or days) inhabiting the object of our scientific methods. Extraneous contact degrades any form of control. Our footprints or the fingerprints we leave on the bannister must be clearly differentiated from the marks left by the original residents of this house. Logic is not sufficient to avoid confusing our own frustration and angst with the victims': we need something else. It's an exhausting intellectual exercise. We're only human: from time to time we amuse ourselves with vain pastimes. The other day, in the garbage (despite having been purified by white spatter patterns, the house is still a monumental trash heap), we found a cardboard box containing hundreds of transparent spinning tops. We guessed that the collection had belonged to a child (possibly dead; a child who was killed within these very walls). We put aside the tweezers, cameras, and precision rulers to sit on the floor and spin tops. We watched them dance under the light of our flashlights, placed bets, and held tournaments until the room was, in forensic terms, a dunghill.

Some of the investigators have tried snorting or smoking the white powder covering the kitchen furniture. They grind the substance finely with a teaspoon or dice it with a credit card, form it into icy lines on the tabletop or the stove, inhale it through rolled bills . . . they say it helps them bear the suffocation of our interminably long working days. We don't believe them. We've even wondered if they are infiltrators: murderers who have come among us with the mission of draining the syntax of this crime scene. As a powder, the white spatter loses its maplike dimension. It no longer tells us a story, and becomes an unstable, volatile flow: something capable of penetrating our bodies. An entity with a terrifying similarity to the music.

4

An elderly man was walking in the garden. Someone said he must be one of us: one of us who had evolved into a state where his only option was to defy the music. No: scientists of that age and demeanor don't do fieldwork; they stay safe in their offices while we, the youngest and least skilled, are sent to lay claim to the evidence that they later use to display their minor genius. So, no, that's not it.

The elderly man made his way through the palm trees and other flora with inhuman grace, as if rather than walking he was circling above the ground to the sound of the music—which at that moment was particularly awful: the constant tone of a busy telephone line with groaning in the background and superimposed explosions. And, incredibly, he was smiling; his wrinkled visage was like those faces children make by pulling down the corners of their eyes with their fingertips and lifting their cheeks with the palms of their hands. Still rotating on his axis, his arms open wide, he was smiling when a branch suddenly broke off from the trunk of a tree and, with the precision of an industrial blade, sliced him in two. There was no blood: just pieces of skin and viscera that, in the asepsis of distance, gleamed like latex.

Someone pointed out that it was our duty as medical forensic assistants to go out into the garden, gather the remains of the body, and add that scene to the remit of the one we'd been assigned to investigate. Someone else laughed aloud. The rest of us moved away from the windows and returned to our spinning-top tournament in another room.

5

We decided by unanimous vote to dismantle this crime scene until not a single brick was left standing. It's a procedure with no juridical basis but infused with perfect logic: destroying the residence is the only viable strategy for halting the degradation of its evidence. Lacking a preconceived plan, we simply exploited the situation as we found it: we snorted the powder in the kitchen, scarred the floors with spinning-top tournaments, devoured the whitewash on the walls . . . Until one of us realized what was happening and said: *We're bona fide science students; we need to design a project.* After that we drew diagrams, handed out hammers, chisels, and tweezers.

It's going to be an arduous process. It might take us the rest of our lives or what remains of our working day. It's an aggressive plan but destruction has its own music. Soon we'll be free: when the walls fall and the ceilings of the crime scene we're investigating finally give way and descend on our heads. We're ashamed to admit it, but we're content: our science is beginning to evolve into a religion.

NEETS

The sweetness that fascinates, the pleasure that kills.
Baudelaire

My son comes to visit and decides to stay for dinner. I ask him what he's been up to and he replies: The usual stuff. I find him almost unbearable: he's twenty-eight and works with his mother for an NGO connected to the LGBTQ community. As far as I'm concerned, you're a NEET, I tell him. This doesn't annoy him. He's always patient with me. He hands over one hundred Preciss condoms sponsored by the WHO and says all I have to do in return is complete an anonymous questionnaire. Why does he humiliate me like this? Because his mother hates me? Because today is my sixtieth birthday? Because Vianey, my new wife, is thirty years younger than me and pregnant? Because I earn a living sleeping, or pretending to sleep, with sick people? I don't deserve this. I'm no prostitute; I'm a conceptual artist who has exhibited his work in five international biennials.

Vianey makes a salad. I protest, say I'll phone for fried chicken, but she says, No, fatso, remember your cholesterol. Goddamn killjoy. There's a reason every hummingbird that crosses her path dies.

At first we thought it was a good omen. That's what her brother

Nazario said. He was lying flat out in front of the TV in our living room (another NEET: he's supposedly on a long-term sabbatical from his nontenured lectureship at some gringo university) when a hummingbird flew in. Nazario watched it wing its way through the house; he said the creature was flapping like an Olympic athlete on speed until it reached the room where my wife was having a siesta, and came to rest on her swollen belly, at which point Vianey woke. According to Nazario, she looked disoriented. The hummingbird didn't move. Vianey was going to shoo it away but Nazario held up his hands to stop her. He said, Sh, it's a sign, it's your baby's *nahual,* its spirit. Vianey lay there quietly for a few seconds. Then the hummingbird toppled from her belly to the mattress and onto the floor. Dead. So far Vianey and her baby have killed about seven of the tiny birds. They have become a silent machine of destruction.

While we're eating the salad, my son asks if I'm still picking up women at the Nuestra Señora de las Pruebas Shelter. I explain that I don't "pick up" anyone: I hire prostitutes who are HIV positive to make gonzo porn movies in which I costar. And no, I haven't gone back there for months, but I'll have to soon; I've just been invited to exhibit in San Francisco. My son chews his salad, turns down his mouth, and says: I think your movies are disgusting, Dad. I feel the urge to stroke his hair. Me, too, son; that's my reply. The truth is that Vianey makes delicious salads.

I started out as a photographer covering gory stories in the *nota roja*, but I discovered my sexual orientation much earlier, possibly when I was still in nursery school and used to go to the park with my grandma. I was unaware that I was working—without being paid—but ever since then I've dedicated myself to studying animals that have recently died or are on death's door. I've never literally killed one, not even a fly. That's what my friends, my siblings, my parents, and my teachers did. Enthralled by the sight, all I did was carefully inspect the remains of their massacres: cockroaches trampled underfoot or drowned in the toilet bowl; ants dissolving in a drop of hydrochloric acid; mice writhing in traps made of metal and wood; decapitated hens running in circles.

Since childhood I've been capable of perceiving the eroticism of damaged bodies. My thing isn't killing but the altered mental states arising from observation. That's why I've never learned to drive, even though my specialty was car crashes: bodies propelled through the thick glass of windshields onto pounds of asphalt, steel, and fluorescent paint. The first time one of my photos—there was something of Francis Bacon in that portrait of a woman with her face splattered over the steering wheel—was printed in large format and hung in the Fruitmarket Gallery in Edinburgh, I spent half my fee on two hookers from the Blue Moon. My hard-on was painful—it takes me twice as much effort to deal with my priapism when there's a camera or more than two people in the room—so I paid them a serious sum in sterling just to watch them tipping the velvet. Take it easy, I ordered. Go at it gently, softly. There was a strange and powerful moment when it occurred to me that this was my way of knocking on both their doors simultaneously and offering them flowers.

Despite the fact that I'm considered technically accomplished, I feel absolutely no affection for photography. For decades I practiced it in the capitalist spirit: a cheap technology that can produce an impression with relative ease and has immediate financial rewards; the fast food of the art market. And neither cinema nor video seems to me any better. Quite the reverse: it's almost impossible to separate cinematic effect from obscenity. Even in the early days that was true. Why did people run from improvised movie theaters when the Lumières' train approached? Why is the animated postcard of workers leaving their factory so hypnotic? Because they are surfaces on which obscenity (phallic in the former case, vaginal in the latter) consumes everything else. If asked, I'd have to confess that all the conceptual artists I know are, at heart, devoted draftsmen. But that observation might perhaps be too tenuous to counter the hatred of the robust spirits who feed mainstream art criticism in the Morlock era of Avelina Lésper & Co.

My move from photography to video wasn't a matter of precision but of acrobatics. When I was in high school, I got hooked on unicycles, stilts, and the trapeze. It was my version of rebellious obedience: my father forced me to take part in the pentathlon, so, as a way of being contrary without creating major conflict, somewhere around '78 I enrolled in one of those profusely intellectual circuses that used to perform in homes, going from one party to the next, in exchange for a little marijuana. Despite my age, I'm still in good shape. From time to time I work out on the bars and rings, and now that our very sensible mayor has installed a cycle path, I can ride five miles on my unicycle without having to dismount. I'm a healthy old bastard.

I gave up my various addictions while still young. At the age of twenty-five I landed in the hospital, suffering from depression. My liver had been destroyed by alcohol, my kidneys were as red as fetuses from the drugs, and my uric acid levels were sky-high due to all that pork I ate. I've been looking after myself ever since. I'm a teetotaler and a militant gymnast. Two years ago my cholesterol started rising again and dull-as-a-dishrag Vianey decided we needed to bring it back down with a diet of lettuce.

The circus and that toxic debacle taught me how to put my body on the line. It's a lesson I forgot for years. Or rather, for years my only way of seeing was through a rearview mirror: my acclaimed photographic portraits of people destroyed in car crashes. At that time my sexuality was exultant. Abstinence is like a dome of excess where all the fantasies of resentful desire end up. Touching bodies, weighing their levels of vitality and mortality: it's the most perfect form of love. And I made love to fat, thin, and old women; to teenagers obsessed by the almond scent of their own anuses on the fingers they licked; to skeletal women whose clitorises had more bite than pure chlorophyll; to divorcées who knew exactly when you should stop moving; to travelers with a talent for invoking the ghost of another man in your body; to very short housewives who warned you from the outset that they are not going to suck your dick; to prostitutes conscious of the moral superiority their salaries gave them; to first-time orgasmers whose gratitude was deeply embarrassing; to beautiful blondes whose good manners made the whole thing feel like a sneeze; to actresses who came without moaning, looking at you obliquely through a fire . . . I made love to healthy women. That was my defect.

I'd had it up to the back teeth with selling monumental front-page tabloid images to art dealers and gallery managers. But more than anything, I hated having my passions so compartmentalized: sex in one place, acrobatics in another, and in a third vector—static, with no direction, severed from everything I thought real—my ability to register how a body is born into the state of grace of putrefaction. It was immediately clear to me that the only area where I could bring these three mysteries together was gonzo porn. My first option was necrophilia. I even managed to practice it on a couple of occasions. There's no human experience beyond the reach of a bribe. The advantage of the dead was that they took my acrobatic spirit to the limits of improbability, particularly since I had to perform with a Sony HVR-V1U in one hand. But an insoluble aesthetic problem arose: I had to fake even the mildest expression of desire. The worst part isn't the lack of an erection: Cialis solves that. It's breaking a taboo and getting nothing more than boredom in exchange.

The HIV hooker thing was a revelation I owe to my ex. She was, as usual, bending my ear about sexual ethics (I hate LGBTQ activists: they are all just closet nuns). She said: You can't go around doing those acrobatics without a rubber (the thing is that I've never liked condoms; my infidelities were unprotected). That was the moment when I decided to get a divorce. My NEET son was still living at home, but he was an adult, so that was no big deal. The problem was battling with my then wife, who is so responsible, serious, and mature that intellectually she's stuck—I suspect—at the age of nine.

In no time at all I was outlining my project to the Sistema Nacional de Creadores de Arte: I was going to fuck seropositive women and film our sexual encounters. It was the only way I could think of to add a touch of eroticism to insipid latex. I was instantly admitted to the network and, in addition, earned thousands of dollars on the international media art circuit. What man wouldn't want to walk through the doors of the Museo Reina Sofía with the stealthy excitement of someone sneaking into a small-town porno theater?

I'm in the dark, projecting photographs of candidates for my next series onto the wall. Vianey bursts in, clearly upset, her eyes moist: they shine in the bright light of the projector. In her hand is the body of a hummingbird. Vianey is a lapdog. A pregnant lapdog. She says: Oh no, this poor thing's dead too. I reply, So what do you want me to do about it? Can't you see I'm working? Put it in the garbage.

I push her out of my studio, close the door, and turn the key.

It's a lie: I'm not working. It's been months since I last enjoyed the gestation of my pieces. I produce mechanically. I am, in the least praiseworthy sense of the expression, a procrastinator of my own orgasms. I'm a NEET too. Just like Vianey and Nazario, just like my son, like the whole fucking world: I don't exist and I don't produce. I hate having to put on the rubber and, at the risk of damaging my health, enter pleasingly curvaceous bodies that, in the end, are nothing more than virus soup: the castoffs of a language. I'm no longer doing it for the aesthetics. Not even for the politics. I'm doing it for the money.

There was a time when Vianey was my votive offering; the Eucharistic body of my greatest creations. I didn't have to go looking for her: she turned up at my home with a CV, the lab report showing she is HIV positive and wearing a lacy top, a blazer, and a red miniskirt. She'd studied at the San Carlos Art Academy but had dropped out. She'd worked as an assistant to Carlos Amorales, had done a residency in Los Angeles under Mario García Torres, and boasted of having once, in her adolescence, slept with Gabriel Orozco. She was a conceptual-art groupie; an intelligent, beautiful twenty-something with a vagina dentata that secretes poison. What more could a manly man washed up on the humiliating shoreline of old age ask for?

We made eighteen gonzo-porno-AIDS movies together. And with the profits we bought a house. Vianey planted gladioli and purple morning glories in the garden.

We haven't had sex for a couple of months. In part this is because the antiretroviral treatment based on Zidovudine and Indinavir produces spectacular bouts of nausea. But it's also because she's just about ready to give birth and her clitoris is so beleaguered by her guts that she climaxes in a matter of seconds. And it's also in part because of how much I hate myself through her because of those dead hummingbirds. Is it her fault that she's got a bird of ill omen in her belly? I'm the guilty party for having chosen to create and procreate in the language of death. As Mallarmé, that indisputable prince of NEETS, said, "Destruction was my Beatrice." My semen is a cemetery.

The first time we filmed together (I say "we filmed" because Vianey was never content to be merely present on set: she'd grab the camera and take shots of me to demonstrate the irrationality of my acrobatic pleasure, of my skirting around the edges of her deadly infection with no defense other than 0.03 millimeters of polyurethane), something was established between us, something profound, more important than the disease or the bitter scent of the vulcanized sheath: we were in love. We've always, ever since that first time, been in love. And everything (the sex, the profits, the image, the curatorship of five international biennials, the flagrant imbecility of Avelina Lésper, the dead birds) has been transformed into horror since we've become what radical art should never be but ends up being in spite of the people who make it: emotion.

I don't know how she got pregnant. I never removed the rubber. She tells me the baby's mine and I believe her. But even so, I can't call it "ours." The odds of it being born with the curse of acquired immunodeficiency syndrome doesn't allow me that luxury. When she told me, I had myself tested and I'm not infected. That isolates me from them. That and the hummingbirds. Something in the internal force of my second child is killing the symbols of the sweetness, velocity, and fragility of the world. I lie awake at night thinking that my need to observe and my loved one's suffering will soon give birth to Death: not simply a sick human being but an entity that destroys everything it touches. A Romantic extermination machine. I used to believe that I was free of such superstitions. Nevertheless, I've spent nine months suffocating under the sublime pillows of German idealism. Dammit.

—

I've come to the conclusion that God is a NEET. It's not so much that he doesn't exist, but that he has been switched off. Someone, in the Dark Night of Time, blindly tripped over the cable and disconnected him. What we learn of Evil enlightens us for a few short moments, like a match that quickly burns out between our fingers. But reality is still a darkened bedroom, and inside that room we all possess hidden animals.

—

The day has arrived. We'd booked it a month in advance. The birth is going to be by cesarean section. The gynecologist tried to refuse me access to the operating room for security reasons, but I changed his mind with a simple gesture: I showed him my CV, my awards, the letter confirming I was a member of the Sistema Nacional de Creadores de Arte; fetishes that give me the title of Honorary Platonic Aids Sufferer.

We spend the whole day in the clinic. My son, my ex-wife, and a couple of journalists drop in to see us. I've drawn the curtains, closed the windows, put down the blinds; expensive clinics like this have gardens, and it's spring: where there's a garden, there are also hummingbirds, naive warriors that Vianey's unborn child frizzles as if they were mosquitoes flying around a cobalt-blue light bulb.

We go into the OR at midday. First I have to don my disguise: a nurse helps me put on a pale blue gown, a plastic hairnet, surgical gloves, a mask... Before doing this, I wash my upper torso. Although immaculately clean, the luxurious bathroom where I carry out these sanitary procedures reminds me of something you might find in an abattoir. It must be that subtle stink. The clinical smell of blood. A ferrous body odor dowsed in boiling water.

When I come out, Vianey doesn't recognize me in my doctor's guise: she looks at me with that detached, ecstatic sweetness you can bestow only on another human when you've been internally dispossessed. I don't recognize her either: I know it's Vianey because the disjointed geometry of her body—for a second I recall the shattered organisms I used to photograph during my car crash days—has her face. But it's as if the photo of a sado-porn model had been stuck over the portrait of your first high school girlfriend. I take her hand and we know each other. We are anything at all: a thing that's still alive. Naturally, I haven't brought my video camera today; that would have been in poor taste.

The operation lasts over an hour. The gynecologist, the virologist, the anesthesiologist, the nurses, the pediatrician: every one of them the best that a famous contemporary artist vanquished by Reality can afford. Among the thousands of people I've seen lately, they are the only ones that don't look to me like crappy little NEETS.

My baby suddenly exits from its mother's belly; the doctor shakes it and it responds with its first war cry. Is it a healthy cry? An ordinary cry? A contagious cry? I won't know until they do the analysis.

The gynecologist passes the tiny body to the young pediatrician. She cradles it, cleans it conscientiously, puts what looks like a white gnome-hat on its head. Then she carries it to the scale and puts a gigantic stethoscope to its chest while Vianey's abdomen is being sutured. The pediatrician turns to me and says, Well, the heart seems fine. Suddenly, she leans against the steel operating table and falls to her knees. Sorry, she says. Give me a moment, I feel terribly dizzy. For an instant I believe my worst fears have been realized: the hummingbirds were just an omen, a rehearsal; Vianey and I have conceived the Exterminating Angel. With lucid madness, I wait for all those wise Galens in their ridiculous gowns to drop dead around me, one by one. I wait my turn for the Void to tear me, too, from this disgusting uncertainty . . .

But the pediatrician's dizzy spell passes. Today isn't the Last Judgment. So I'll have to bear the burden of this anguish for at least one more night. The doctor places the newborn in my hands. I say to that scrap of flesh: How are you doing, you frigging NEET? How are you doing, my prince, my pinch of sugar, my little ninja, my sun? And I stroke his ears and tiny toes.

Then they snatch him from me and take him away to carry out the necessary retroviral tests.

The Roman Wedding

For Saíd Herbert

There isn't a single car left in the Cadereyta prison parking lot, and the sun is beating down like a bottle-blow to the head. We park in the last space in a triangle formed by a concrete wall, a patch of open ground, and the security hut, get out of the Cutlass, sign the pig's logbook, and walk along a narrow corridor between chrome chain-link fences topped with razor wire. An hour later we see him coming. We recognize him in the distance as he passes through the second gate.

"Looks like he's been soaked in Fab," says Nelson.

"Shut it."

"Like they used lashings of it. He's more washed-out and faded than the ghost of Don Manos. God rest his soul."

I dodge behind to punch him in the ribs. Nelson's six-foot-ten frame doubles over as if I'd hurt him. Bebito passes through the last two gates, I go to meet him, and we hug, Nelson catches up, hugs us both in his clumsy-bear way, and we return to the parking lot, our arms still linked across one another's shoulders. There are pigs every few yards along the corridor, and you don't open your mouth around pigs. We climb into the Cutlass in silence. Nelson is at the wheel with Bebito in the passenger seat. I'm in the back.

"Who came up with the coin?" asks Bebito as soon as we close the doors.

"Uncle Chapete. A present from Maruca."

"Fucking old bat. Her and Urko."

"Urko's taking care of the funeral."

"How much did they give you?"

"A hundred thou."

"Miserable tightasses."

"You got it, man. It came to eighty. You want change?"

Bebito looks at me in the rearview mirror. His eyes are brimming with tears.

"Hey, you're my bro. When have I ever asked for change?"

This makes me smile: I haven't had a contract for three weeks. That twenty thousand will get me through the month. Then I remember that my father's body is lying waiting for someone to wash it, apply makeup, dress it in a suit and tie, and all my enthusiasm evaporates.

"You're looking good," says Nelson, his hands gripping the wheel while we wait for a truck loaded with Montemorelos oranges to pass before we join the traffic on the Monterrey highway.

Bebito lowers the window and looks at himself in the side mirror.

"I'm lean as a hare. Four months in general population just because Urko didn't see why he should pay for privileges. They beat me to a pulp."

We pull in to a gas station. Bebito tells Nelson to grab some beer and smokes from the OXXO store, then gets out of the car and starts clowning around by my window: he takes off his T-shirt to show off the muscles he forged during his year in lockup. Nelson returns, Bebito puts his tee back on, they both take their seats up front, Nelson starts the Cutlass, Bebito lights a Marlboro, opens a Tecate, and offers me a can. I shake my head.

"You seen him yet?"

"Pop? No."

"Who found the body?"

"Your brother."

"Muñeco?"

"Mhm."

"He's your brother too."

"Says he ain't."

Bebito takes a swig from his can.

"That's Urko, dude. Wants us at each other's throats."

I meet his eyes in the mirror.

"It's not Urko. Muñeco's pissed off with me about the rock."

"I'll tell the asshole not to hold grudges."

"No sweat. Anyway, I'm headed back to Zacatecas tomorrow."

Bebito unfastens his seat belt and turns to me, his cheek resting on the upholstery.

"Got any gear?"

"Nope."

"I do," says Nelson.

He passes over a small bag and the cap of a pen that he's extracted from his armpit. Bebito takes a snort and looks at me again in the mirror.

"No gear, no beer. You down on your luck or what?"

"I get by," I answer in English.

"But why? Have you gotten yourself into a group or some shit like that?"

"I've been going to Narcotics Anonymous for a year and a half."

"Where?"

"Zacatecas."

He takes two more snorts, sucks back the snot, clears his throat, passes the bag back to Nelson, and twists his body around so he's looking me straight in the face.

"Congratulations, bro. That takes balls. Truth is, you were pissing outside the pot."

Nelson is engaged in a duel with a truck driver who doesn't signal, slows down at curves, but then speeds up when we try to pass.

"Fucker."

"Yeah."

We drive on in silence. When we finally overtake the truck, my brother warns:

"You were way out of line when you filched that piece of rock from Muñeco. The filth took him for a ride and beat the shit out of him."

"He told me."

"Pop said he wasn't gonna kill you, 'cause you're flesh and blood, but when he saw you, he was gonna put a slug in your ass."

I don't respond. Nelson laughs and cries at the same time. Then Bebito starts. Then I do: the three of us know that I'll never talk to my father again, that my father is never gonna put a slug in my ass.

"So what are you doing?"

"I've got a maintenance business."

"Maintaining what?"

"Whatever comes my way: plumbing, construction, wiring, painting houses, waxing floors. I just bought a buffer."

"You always liked having something to do. Don Manos used to say, 'Why don't you follow your elder brother's example, you bunch of wasters?' even to Urko, and he's not his son."

Nelson suddenly brakes to avoid rear-ending a Cherokee. The traffic is slowing down to a walking pace.

"Are you doing OK?"

"Unclogging pipes and waxing floors? Can't complain. But after a whole life spent selling shit, the odd centavo here and there doesn't make a big impression."

"And what did you do with it?" asked Nelson, squeezing in on the motor on the left in second gear.

"With what?"

"The rock."

"I smoked it. What do you think?"

"The whole lot?"

"Well, yeah. You think I'd have joined Narcotics Anonymous otherwise?"

The traffic comes to a standstill around Parque Fundidora.

"Sorry. It's rush hour," says Nelson. "I'll try to turn off onto Colón."

Bebito opens another Tecate.

"Muñeco found him."

"Yeah, that's right. I'm not sure just how it happened. Your mom talked to my old lady, and she told me. They say he had a heart attack in the bathroom."

"Shitting."

"Washing his hands, they said."

"Because of the soda."

"No. They say he'd stopped."

"Not a fucking thing since he came out of the can," Nelson added. "I know 'cause I offered him a fix and he came this close to giving me a thrashing. It was like the thing had gotten to him, man. He was in general population too. We put up the money for privileges, but the kid they had as minister of public security wouldn't take it. Seems like what we got was a lesson from the state. They took your old man out every day and whacked his nuts. Why d'ya think the old man let the AGO take the houses and the cars? You think he'd have done that if they hadn't had him by the balls?"

We turn on Colón and down to Guerrero.

"Take the next turn after Diagonal."

"What?"

"Here, dude."

"But the funeral par—"

"I wanna drop by the Roman Wedding first."

Nelson takes another right and we rejoin Guerrero at the wall with mirrored plasterwork. He then takes a left and we cross the Treviño neighborhood on Marco Polo as far as Vidriera. We park in front of the Roman Wedding, the disputed cantina that once belonged to my pop. There are "closed" signs on all the doors and in the windows. The pockmarks left by AK-47s on the facade blend in with areas of fifteen or twenty layers of peeling paint.

"Frigging Urko."

"It wasn't him." Nelson plucks up the courage to contradict him. "He was in the bar that day. You think he was going to order all that gunfire on himself?"

Bebito gives him a backhanded slap.

"What the fuck do you know about anything, you knucklehead? Your brains are in your dick."

Nelson nods. I inspect him covertly. The graying hair is new. I remember him as a colossal figure heading balls into the opposing goal during Llanos games in Asarco Park when I was a kid.

"Urko told the filth," says Bebito. "Why d'ya think they picked me up? The two-timing rat prefers to offer his loyalty to the assholes who lost the war than to take over the pitch."

"Sorry, Bebito," says Nelson.

"And what's all that shit about no bribes? When did you last hear of a damn screw not taking a bribe? Urko just said that to keep them quiet while he was fucking up Pop."

"You're right," replies Nelson, and switches on the ignition of the Cutlass.

Tony is standing at the top of the wide, crowded steps leading up from the sidewalk. You can hear him shouting halfway down the street. As we drive past the funeral parlor, I open the window to get a clear picture of what's going on. The well-dressed fatso guarding the entrance is dragging hard on one of his ears, seemingly trying to pull it off, as Tony pokes an index finger into his chest. A couple of steps below, Muñeco stands smoking.

Nelson joins the line of cars waiting to enter the parking lot. I see Uncle Chapete by a public telephone. He's wearing a black suit, his arms are crossed, and he's murmuring a prayer, looking blankly into the distance.

We park, get out of the Cutlass. The shapely calves of three plump little miniskirted cousins pass by. Our remaining men (no more than eight) move aside to make way for us. They are wearing off-the-rack black suits bought at the last minute in Del Sol or El Nuevo Mundo. We come across Iris: she looks awful, teetering back and forth across the entrance to the parking lot. She's wearing a short, strapless mourning dress that hugs her boobs and her perfect high-class-restaurant-hostess's glutes.

"Tell him to forget the ass licking," she says as Bebito, Nelson, and I pass. "He was my old man, you bastards."

She smells of Camay soap and Mennen peach shampoo.

On the sidewalk, Uncle Chapete greets us with open arms, like he's trying to hug us and, at the same time, stop us from getting past him. His eyes are red; he's been smoking a joint.

"He was only asking us to wait, Pop. Don't be so tough on him."

He likes playing the gangster, but this is a plea.

"Who?" asks Bebito. "Urko?"

"Your little brother Urko, Pop. Don't be so tough on him."

"That asshole ain't my brother."

Bebito bypasses Chapete and walks straight to the steps leading to the chapels. We follow behind. Muñeco watches us approach. He throws down his half-smoked joint, makes a wry face at me, and links his hands behind his back.

"You heard, Bebo? They won't let us in till the son turns up, man. *The son*, for god's sake. That fuckin' fairy's going too far."

Muñeco tries to grab Bebito but Nelson pushes him aside. Bebito ascends the steps to where Tony is still standing, gets him in a wrestling hold, and pulls him down. Tony tries to defend himself, but when he recognizes our brother, he spreads his arms wide in a sign of surrender.

"They won't let me in."

"I know, dude. Me neither. Not even him, and he's the eldest," says Bebito, freeing him and nodding toward me. "No Pipo the Clown stuff, though."

"Fuck that!"

Bebito strokes the back of his neck and kisses him on the cheek.

"I'm just gonna ask one thing, kiddo. Is this how you want your last sight of him to be?"

Marta, Tony's mother, drags her boy off. He's a kind of distant brother: I can't have met him more than ten times max. Don Manos Torpes never wanted him mixed up in the business. He can't be even eighteen: still in school. Tony starts screeching, breaks lose from his mom, and comes back to us. Tony, Bebito, Muñeco, and I sit on the steps to wait for Cousin Urko to turn up so we can go inside and say goodbye to Pop.

A little under ten minutes later, Urko descends from a Land Rover, escorted by his driver, Vic, and a short, well-hung thug he must surely be fucking. After him come Aunt Maruca and Doña Quecha, Bebito and Muñeco's mother.

"I really didn't see that coming, Sultanes," says Bebito with a laugh, mimicking a sportscaster's voice.

I look around and tally up the widows. Only my mom is missing. I suddenly feel I've got nothing to be proud of.

Urko passes Bebito and the other mourners, comes to where I'm standing, and hugs me.

"Sorry, cousin: I told them they had to wait for the eldest son. But they're knuckleheads, and they got us mixed up."

He's wearing a three-quarter-length Dolce & Gabbana leather coat that, in the suffocating summer heat of the New Kingdom of León, makes him look like an elegant Italian gangster and, at the same time, the son of a suburban National Action voter. He's covering his lazy eye with one hand and I notice he's put on weight. Turning to Bebo, he lowers his hand and says, as if speaking to everyone:

"I think the right thing would be for his eldest son to say goodbye to the boss first. Agreed?"

He turns around and, without waiting for a reply, takes my arm and leads me toward the door of the funeral parlor. The others cluster behind us. Iris attempts to get her perfect high-class-restaurant-hostess's figure up front, but Urko elbows her aside, almost knocking her over.

"Fucking sod. He was my man."

Urko covers his lazy eye again so he can look at me with the good one. Just behind us are Maruca, Uncle Chapete, Tony, and his mother, Marta. I look around for Bebo and see him a couple of steps below, with Muñeco and Doña Quecha, his mother, holding an arm apiece, and escorted from on high by six feet, ten inches of Nelson. For no particular reason, I remember that Nelson used to drive us to elementary school. I give Bebo an uncertain look and he blows me a kiss and smiles one of those perfect smiles of his that, along with the latest-model truck, the Buchanans, the Banda music, and the high-caliber weaponry my father used to buy for him, have endowed him with the privilege of fucking the most beautiful asses in the Kingdom.

The well-dressed fatso guard opens both panels of the wooden door to let us pass. Urko and I stumble in, the crush of people forcing us forward. It's dark. A switch clicks on and I hear that refrigerator buzzing of old fluorescent bulbs. Flat light splashes across the floor tiles. At the far end of a long green and coffee-colored room stands the coffin, covered with an array of white, yellow, and purple flowers. Urko drops my arm. At my back, I sense people fanning out, hugging the walls of the chapel as if fleeing death. I smell the nauseating scent of the newly lit candles, hear the first sobs, all of them feigned except for Bebito's; his sound more like snorts and hardened snot. Dry-eyed, I walk to the coffin. Suddenly, I'm ashamed not to be wearing a tie. I think about the morning I first met my father.

I was seven years old and my grandma got me out of bed (it wasn't yet light) and delivered me to my mom at the back door of a brothel called El Siglo XX. What I remember most clearly is that Mom's eyelids were covered with some silvery powder that extended to her temples. We took a cab and she removed her makeup with Theatrical Cold Cream as we drove to a place on Calle Villagrán for an Eskimo juice. The sun was just coming up when we saw him on the other side of the street. He was setting up a stand selling heavy-metal T-shirts.

"Say hi to your father," she said.

Mom swears to this very day that we met by pure chance, but I know she'd planned it: she'd fallen for some guy who couldn't stand my being around and was pressing her to do something about it. Two months later I moved into the house belonging to Manos Torpes: that's what everyone in the neighborhood called my father because he could lift a two-pint Carta Blanca in one hand as if it were half that size. His fists were as powerful as those of the great Julio César Chávez and his fingers and palms more solid than the Blue Demon's.

Years later I helped him run the retail narco trade in Treviño. They used to call me Manitas, little hands. But although I was the oldest, for Pop I was never the firstborn son. That status belonged to Bebito: my father had actually married his mother, Doña Quecha. We all knew it and respected his decision. Except, it would seem, Urko.

I kneel on the wooden prie-dieu with satin cushions so that my head is only just above his, resting in horizontal comfort—or at least that's how it looks—in the open coffin. He's still the most handsome bastard I've ever seen in my life. The fags at the funeral parlor haven't dared to spoil his face: barely a touch of makeup. He has a neatly cut salt-and-pepper beard, marked crow's-feet, a finely shaped nose and mouth, and the scar of a knife wound crossing his left eye. My old man is beautiful. I want to kill him. I want to kiss him on the lips.

Around noon the next day, after the burial, Bebito makes us stop for tacos before going to the wake.

"We show up last and together," he commands.

Marta, Tony's mother, tries to stop her son from coming with us, until Bebito swears on Don Manos's memory that it's for his own safety, that nothing's going to happen and that we'll keep an eye on the beers. In the taqueria, Nelson and I sit at a separate table so as not to rile Muñeco. Then we pile into the Cutlass and head for the Roman Wedding.

"Take Avenida Carranza," Bebito barks at Nelson.

Tony, Muñeco, and I are crowded into the back seat. Muñeco is pressed up against the window to avoid even touching me, as though I had mange. From time to time he looks over his shoulder, like he wants to put a bullet in me.

"Here," says Bebito.

We park on Magallanes, the street that runs along the back of the cantina, and open the windows to smoke. The whole block is empty. There's a red-hot-coal breeze, the sort that issues from the mouth of Monterrey in the summer. The only sound to be heard is the faint voice of Lalo Mora singing "Eslabón por eslabón." We all smoke our own cigarettes.

"I want a shooter," says Tony.

"What d'ya mean, a frigging shooter, you chickenshit sniveler? It's a funeral, not a job!"

"So why not go in through the front door, like everyone else?"

Bebito doesn't answer.

We scale the outside of Norma's place, Nelson first, then Bebito and Tony. I bring up the rear. Muñeco has to be helped because he's out of shape. Then we sit on the roof while Nelson runs along a couple of walls and descends into the yard via the Conchis's house. While waiting, we do target practice, throwing pebbles at the wall of the adjoining building. It's almost four, the sun is beating down like a bottle-blow to the head, it's really hot, and that's why I take off my shirt. After around fifteen minutes, there's a whistle. I walk right to the edge of the roof. Nelson waves from the backyard of the Roman Wedding, holding a one-ounce bag of coke. We climb down the wall. Vic, Urko's driver, comes out to meet us.

"Not real trusting, are you?"

No one answers.

Inside, Lalo Mora is still playing, and there are two-pint bottles of Buchanan's 18 from Costco, small bags of coke, and six-by-eight-inch mirrors on all the tables; in the kitchen, Bro is working his ass off making carnitas tacos; by the jukebox, there's a high stool with a red cushion and piles of ten-peso coins: everything just the way Manos Torpes wanted it. Fucking Urko, he didn't even forget the

Bulgarian girls from Don Raciel Pulido's club, who right now are looking bored, dancing without poles in garish jumpsuits.

I put my shirt back on. Tony leans over a couple of lines, sniffs like a pro, and no one stops him: he's fucking around, I think: fucking his mother, Marta. Muñeco, Bebito, and Nelson are sharing a table. I walk over to the end of the bar nearest the front door, where my cousin Urko and his shaved-headed, cocksucking thug are dishing out. Urko passes me a tortilla.

"We've just had tacos," I say by way of apology.

Urko's mouth turns down, as if he's shrugging his shoulders, and he slides the plate along the bar and the thug catches it. My cousin's lazy eye twitches again: he covers it with his hand. He's taken off the Dolce & Gabbana coat and is now wearing a bright red chef's uniform with a hat that has white skulls on a black background. We all know he's not the one doing the cooking.

"Are you going to stay on?"

I shake my head. Urko grabs the back of my neck and pulls me toward him over the bar as though he's going to kiss me. He keeps his other hand over his lazy eye. His breath smells of Listerine.

"Stay, dude. Stay here beside me a little while, now that you're clean."

"Word gets around."

"Bebito's full of shit, but you know what my pop wanted."

"He wasn't your pop."

"He wanted them out of the business. For their own safety."

"You never called him Pop."

"That's why he made me his second-in-command. I need you to keep that pack of hounds under control, dude. You know them. They're good kids, but they don't see the big picture. They don't see the opportunities."

"And I do, right? Because I fucked my nose up with coke."

"That's not what we're talking about."

Disappointed, he lets go of my neck and returns to the kitchen for more tortillas.

I order a mineral water, ask for a deck of cards, and play solitaire at the bar. Someone has turned off the jukebox without my even noticing. At the back of the room, the mothers are praying. Vic passes me on his way out into the street.

"Tell your cousin I'll be in the wagon, will ya?"

I nod. When Vic opens the door, I glance outside. It's beginning to get dark.

Iris is now sitting next to Bebito. She's drunk as a skunk and snorting coke from the table with the long nail of her little finger, getting right up close to my brother's face when she talks and brushing knees with him under the table. Urko's thug turns to me with a smile.

"The old girl's already looking for a replacement."

Urko slaps him and says something I don't catch. I'm not sure if that slap is just for my benefit, but everyone in the family knows Iris is a twin, and she always gets up close like that when she's talking, always, ever since she was a girl and we were all fantasizing about fucking her when she was a little older, never thinking that the one to win the prize would be our father. Even Urko imagined fucking her, and he doesn't really like broads. We all ended up loving her like a kid sister.

Muñeco sits down next to me at the bar.

"Since when did you play solitaire, dude?"

I tell him the truth:

"It's just my way of laughing in the face of temptation. Of not having a line. I'll be on my way soon."

"You should've laughed in that face earlier, you asshole. You could've saved me the beating of a lifetime."

"I know, dude."

We sit there in silence for a while: I'm concentrating on my game and he's sipping his drink.

"At least I have the consolation of knowing you never got to say goodbye to my boss," he eventually observes.

Then, like someone carrying the Olympic torch of another guy's wound, he picks up his glass and disappears into the crowd.

He's wrong.

A couple of months before they threw Manos Torpes in jail (around four months after I'd stopped smoking rock, begun going to NA, and started working in maintenance), he'd called me on my cell phone. He said my mother had given him the number.

"How you doing?"

"Fine."

I thought: He wants to kill me. That's why he called.

He didn't mention the brick of rock I took with me when I fled the Kingdom.

"I'm here in Zacatecas, son. I need you to do me a little favor."

He said he'd been driving from Guadalajara with an average load when he got a tip-off that they were going to take him at the Marine checkpoint. He said he'd pulled in at the roadside, buried four pounds of coke and a few bottles, and driven on to the checkpoint. The naval guys made him get out of the car, frisked him, roundly dissed him, and almost took the wagon to pieces but, not finding anything, had unwillingly let him go. He said he was in Zacatecas without any dough or goods, shitting his pants from the shock, and that all he wanted was to get a fix to lower the stress level and continue on his way. He was in rival territory, he said, and there was no way he could pick up the stuff personally, for fear of being recognized and turned in, he had no money, so please would I do him a little favor and speak to the dealers, because it's not like I was anyone important. It all sounded like some bizarre story to get me out of my home ground and give me that slug in the ass or a planking, but . . . What could I do? It was my father on the other end of the line. I gave him my address, hung up, and called the number of the best dealer in the city: Manos Torpes never used poor-quality goods.

We were together for less than five minutes. Since he didn't want to enter the building, he parked on the corner and asked me to come out to hand over the merchandise. I climbed into the front passenger seat beside him, feeling scared shitless. He looked even more paranoid than I felt. When I'd closed the door, he gave me a slap that almost took my head off. That's when I was sure he wasn't going to kill me: it was the nicest gesture of affection he was capable of showing.

"What's up, you bastard? Your mom told me you joined NA."

I felt ridiculous saying yes, it was true, as I slid an eight ball of coke across the seat. Pop took the bag, did two key bumps, and then sat in silence, waiting for the stuff to take effect. He nodded approvingly. But he never once, during the whole conversation, looked me in the eyes.

"So," he said, holding out his right hand, "as the elephant said to the ant: 'Bless your soul and fuck off to some other hole.'"

I couldn't bear it any longer.

"I love you, Pop."

He nodded his approval once more without looking at me. We shook hands.

"Better now than when I'm dead," he said.

I got out of the pickup. As he pulled away, I caught a glimpse of his face. He was crying.

I walk out of the Roman Wedding as though I want to get some air. The only person to catch on to my real intention is Bebito: we look each other straight in the eyes before I cross the threshold, and I think he's going to stop what he's doing and come over, but in the end he just gives a vague gesture of farewell. I return it and leave.

The night's good: the temperature has fallen slightly and there's a breeze that's almost cool, a strange thing in high summer. Standing beside Urko's van, I light a cigarette. Vic is snoring in the driver's seat. I think about how simple it would be to go around the corner to Nelson's unlocked Cutlass, take the automatic he keeps in the glove compartment, return to the door of the Wedding, and shoot Vic first, keeping my free hand over my eyes to protect them from the shards of glass, slip the rod behind my back, go inside, pretending to be alarmed, run to my cousin Urko to explain, put one, two, three bullets into his mug, hand the weapon to Bebito like a scepter ("Say it was the filth"), and leave, never to return.

(I wonder if my father would ever have been capable of doing something similar.)

I think all that in much less time than is needed to write it: less time than you'd need to take a drag on a cigarette. Then I walk along Marco Polo toward Vicente Guerrero in search of a cab to take me to the bus station.

After a few blocks I come across six or seven vagrants swigging Caguamas in a doorway. Two of them step onto the sidewalk, barring my way and looking like their intentions are anything but innocent. I remember that beneath my boxers I'm wearing a money belt holding twenty thousand pesos. I pull up my sleeves and square my shoulders, preparing myself for the blows.

From the darkest corner of the doorway comes a voice:

"Quit it, you morons. It's Manitas."

The two bums move closer. They recognize me—or pretend to—in the shadows and move apart to let me pass.

"Sorry, sir," one of them says.

"My most sincere condolences, Manos Torpes," says the other. Like I was the heir to . . . what? A nickname, nothing more.

I walk to the limits of Treviño, the cars zooming past with their windows down and music blasting out. At the junction of Guerrero and Colón, I turn to take one last look at my neighborhood: a dense darkness sparsely dotted with colored lights. Then I hail a cab and ask to be taken to the bus station. And that's it; that's the last of Monterrey, the last of the Kingdom for me.

There Where We Stood

Did I see him first, or was it Cristina? I'm not completely sure. I do remember that we were tired, hungry, and hadn't slept: we'd taken a red-eye from Mexico to Santiago, and Cris had been detained for an hour at the airport because she forgot to declare a bag of granola at customs (Cristina told me that the very well-groomed, handsome young man from the Chilean agency had asked her if she'd forgotten to declare it before or after she was given the customs form), and then when we got to the hotel, it was the usual thing:

"Very sorry, but your rooms aren't ready yet. Check-in is at midday. In the meantime, we'd like to offer you a courtesy aperitif."

I think I saw him first: we were sipping pisco sours at ten in the morning in the bar of the Panamericana Hotel Providencia, 146 Francisco Noguera, Santiago de Chile, and I was talking about the book I was writing, a *crónica* on the subject of the massacre of the Chinese community in Torreón in 1911, and Cristina was talking about the book she was writing, a lecture-essay-*crónica*-novel on the subject of Juan Rulfo, or something like that, and we got deeply involved in describing black-and-white photos and journeys to Mexico Profundo, to pre-Hispanic Mexico, and discussing the economic history of automobile tire plants in our country (some of them financed by Nazi money; that was where my story and Cristina's overlapped), and I thought: I know that man.

He'd taken a seat a couple of tables away from us. From that distance, he looked quite sober: very smartly dressed with a neat wide knot in his necktie, his slightly wavy hair combed back off his face, a clear brow that was also an alexandrine tercet of wrinkles, pronounced but not heavy bags under his eyes, a cigarette in his downturned mouth, and a gaze that left you unsure if it expressed mere mockery or the desire to kill you. That's Juan Rulfo, I said to myself. And then, idiotically—as if Rulfo was alive or some joker had refused to grant him an exit visa—No way, man. It can't be him. I mean, we're in Santiago.

Cristina was talking about a photograph of a wagon traveling up a steep slope or some oxen or something. She stopped midsentence, looked over my shoulder at the man with the smartly knotted necktie, downed her pisco sour in one gulp, and said:

"Let's go. I'll buy you a drink somewhere else."

"But . . . ," I stammered.

"It's just that he's here again. He never lets me get deep into a conversation."

We stood up and took our drink credits to the cashier. Behind us, Rulfo also got to his feet, and strangely enough, he didn't have that smooth, slightly hoarse voice you hear in his recordings but a rancorous croak with only the slightest of fricative echoes.

"Where are you going? Wait, girl."

Cristina had already passed through the main door of the Panamericana Hotel Providencia and was hailing a cab. I didn't know whether to speed up, as she had done, like someone fleeing from a ghost, or to be polite to the man: after all, he was elderly, my compatriot, and, above all, one of the writers I most admire in the whole world.

Juan Rulfo took advantage of my hesitation to grab my arm: clearly it wasn't me he was interested in, but Cristina. He pulled me close to his chest and said:

"I'm the devil and I love her. Go after the girl and tell her that, please."

Caries

For Valeria Luiselli

One day Ramón Rigual discovered sheet music in his teeth. This was a peculiar but not extraordinary event. At that time, Ramón was a conceptual artist, so he was accustomed to such offbeat occurrences.

Naturally, the first thing he did was visit a dentist. After a brief, thorough routine examination, the dentist declared:

"I haven't seen a case like this in years. You have a very unremarkable yet perfectly rotten set of teeth. And you've never had them checked before?"

Ramón had stopped visiting dentists twelve years before, when a dental assistant had praised the health of his ivories, which she believed could be credited to the very high pH value of his saliva. From that moment on, Ramón lost interest in the annual checkups his mother scheduled.

"Djuno unthin bow mushi?" he politely asked his new dentist.

No, the man knew nothing about music.

So Ramón Rigual gave up on his dental health for the second time. He went out into the street in numb pursuit of the most profound of aesthetic experiences.

His next move would consist of undertaking an objective reconstruction: translating his individual perception of the human and the transcendent into the language of the arts. Opening his mouth very wide, he took a series of digital photographs.

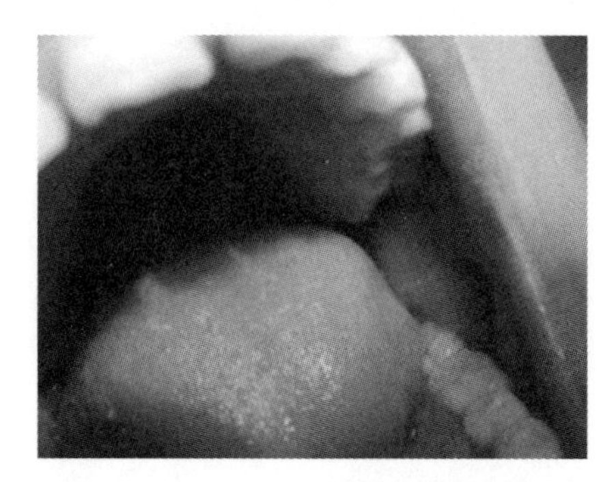

The following step, he decided, would be to learn to read the notes: he'd recognized them as such immediately; deciphering them was another matter. Not only was he illiterate with respect to music, but since his quarrel with Bobo Lafragua, he'd felt a deep disgust for anything to do with the subject: Bobo was, or had been, a music producer, and having to lower himself to the level of a rival seemed to Ramón the greatest of indignities.

He and Bobo had been friends and collaborators for years, and Ramón had even had a cameo in one of the many youthful projects Lafragua initiated but never completed. What led to the final, bitter divorce was their very different attitudes toward originality: Rigual mistrusted retinal art but had a blind faith in his own point of view, in his aesthetic conscience. Lafragua, on the other hand, believed firmly in appropriation, recycling, and pastiche. This divergence became extreme the fourth or fifth time Bobo plagiarized ideas or projects his colleague had mentioned during casual conversations. Furious, Ramón protested. Bobo Lafragua, with a highbrow expression and lowbrow language, replied by paraphrasing his favorite cinema antihero:

"I am your father, you bastard."

The paradox, as Ramón began to realize, was that he was on the verge of achieving fame—he was certain of this: what he had in his teeth was his magnum opus—precisely by means of the unconscious (but well-chewed) drawing of a piece of music. Not by plagiarism but, as Cai Guo-Qiang would say, by "borrowing your enemy's arrows." Bobo Lafragua, he thought, would die of jealousy (the phrase was metaphorical; the desire for such an outcome was not).

After long months of arduous and disciplined study (more than one of his neighbors complained to the tenants' association or snuffled doggedly at the door of his apartment in a run-down building in Doctores, trying to work out if the awful smell was due to an inclement accumulation of trash or a human body in the process of decomposition), Ramón Rigual emerged from his rooms holding a jewel: six sheets of lined paper.

Caries

Music by Ramón Rigual

A-Piano
A-Piano
10
13
16
mf
3

19
A-Piano
A-Piano
22
25
pp

28
A-Piano
A-Piano
31
34
mf

37
A-Piano
A-Piano
40

43
A-Piano
A-Piano
46
49

By that time, his curator had everything ready: in a small, exclusive gallery in the San Miguel Chapultepec neighborhood he had hung—in large format on acrylic—the photos of Rigual's teeth,

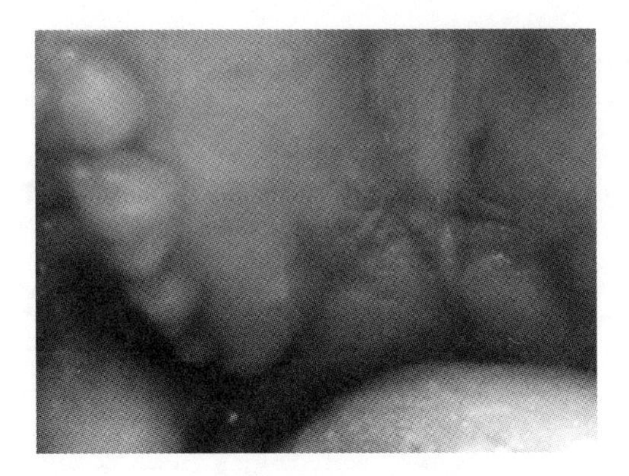

plus the pages of his score. To add the finishing touch to the exhibition, they hired two musicians to play the short piece (barely a minute and a half in duration) forty times during the opening.

The show would have been one of the most stunning parties (read: cultural events) in Mexico City that autumn if it hadn't been for an unfortunate incident. While "Caries" was being played for about the twentieth time, a young music lover in the crowd exclaimed with unshakeable authority,

"I've got it! That's J. Zimmerman's 'All Fours.'"

All Fours

Music by J. Zimmerman

10
A-Piano
mf
A-Piano
3
3
3
3
3
13
16

A-Piano
A-Piano
19
22
25
pp

A-Piano
A-Piano
28
31
34
mf

37
A-Piano
A-Piano
40

43
A-Piano
A-Piano
46
49

Predictably enough, word of the scandal spread much faster and more widely than any artistic work or manifestation could aspire to: "Caries," the masterpiece by the conceptual creator Ramón Rigual, was nothing more than a collection of revolting dental selfies accompanied by the uninspired plagiarism of the best-known piece by a New York disciple of the minimalist composer Steve Reich. Those commenters with the greatest thirst for blood identified two sources of ridicule: the repeated defense of originality that Rigual had expressed over the years in interviews, articles, and panels, which now sounded fraudulent; and the artist's ignorance of music, since, they said, what he'd filched didn't even have the grace of obscurity—it was available on iTunes.

For his part, Ramón suffered less from the public tongue-lashing than from what he considered a betrayal by Nature. If anyone could be certain that no such illegal appropriation had ever occurred, it was he. Yet the document that had emerged from his mouth and Zimmerman's piece were identical down to the last note. Rigual had always opted for a confrontational, even irreverent approach in his modes of expression, but deep down his basic concept of art was not so different from that of the Romantics: uniqueness, creative originality. And pure shit: if this needed daily confirmation, he had only to look at his teeth in the mirror. That image held him so deeply in its spell that it pushed him—in some gradual, subtle way—into the arms of psychosis.

One evening, after spending hours in front of the mirror, poking about in his mouth with a curette, Ramón Rigual broke into the office of the dentist who knew nothing about music, hijacked his surgical equipment, fled back to his decaying apartment in Doctores, and, in an attempt to exorcise from his body the concept of beauty as an idée fixe, he pulled out his teeth one by one. The police officers assigned to investigate the theft found him several hours later, lying on his bed, covered in blood, vomit, and urine. He was sent to a psychiatric clinic.

When he awoke, Rigual recognized at his bedside the features of his former rival Bobo Lafragua, who, stroking his hair, simply said:

"My poor idiotic friend."

The story has a less somber epilogue. On Bobo Lafragua's instructions, Miguel Oriflama, the curator of the exhibition, recovered Rigual's scattered teeth and included them in the catalog of *Whole Garden, Lactose-Free Garden,* a group exhibition of mutilation art at the Monterrey Contemporary Art Museum.

J. Zimmerman flew in from New York to view the remains of a story that had come to his ears in luminously equivocal snippets. The piece itself didn't seem to him particularly impressive. But when he carefully explored the broken teeth, a shiver ran down his spine. In an interview, he described the experience as follows:

"I was able to read the score immediately: only a novice could have missed it. It was perfectly clear to me that the score wasn't mine. Or at least, not at that point. Maestro Rigual's failure was never of an aesthetic nature; it was rhetorical. He transcribed what was written in his mouth in a painfully clumsy manner. What is more unsettling is that, by coincidence, that nonsensical transcription turned out to be identical to one of my works."

In vindication of the Mexican conceptual artist, J. Zimmerman agreed to make a correct transcription of the piece, asking as his only recompense that he be credited as coauthor of the work. As a tribute to his toothless ghostly interlocutor, he called the composition "Curette."

Curette

Music by Zimmerman / Rigual

A-Piano
A-Piano
mf
10
13
16

A-Piano
A-Piano
19
22
25
pp

A-Piano
A-Piano
28
31
34
mf

A-Piano
A-Piano

49

The recording has sold well, especially in the United States. So well that, with a portion of his royalties, J. Zimmerman has been able to buy an expensive present: the complete set of Ramón Rigual's teeth.

The two have now become almost friends (they never speak, just sit opposite each other for hours at a time). Zimmerman brought the teeth back, gift-wrapped. At first Ramón Rigual refused to accept them: he opened the wooden box in which they came and threw the fragments onto the table. J. Zimmerman patiently gathered them in the palm of his hand and imitated Rigual's gesture, casting down the pieces of tooth as if the act were a form of divination. A few hours later, Zimmerman and Rigual embarked on what appears to be a game of dice (it is still in progress and, on certain afternoons, draws us to the table they occupy in this park); they lay their bets in cash, throw the former contents of Ramón Rigual's mouth (he now has dentures) onto the table, and depending on how the decay falls, one of them takes the money in the pot.

The only people in the world who are capable of reading the ciphers formed by the dental fragments are those two men.

(Written in collaboration with Jorge Rangel)

The Dog's Head

I'd found a job as a stocker in Wilhelm-Kabus-Straße. For over two weeks, at rush hour, I boarded the S2 at Südkreuz station, that impersonal bastion of Schöneberg, with its transmodern-whale interior, in which half the world speaks Slovakian, hundreds of signs inform you that you are being filmed, and you can even enjoy a traditional dish called Burger King. Every evening after work I had to travel—unticketed—from the south of Berlin to Pankow, on the northernmost point of the Hundekopf circular line, where I'd pitched my tent: a gay couple had offered me space in their yard when, during a party, I'd shown them how to light the coals of their barbecue in the old Coahuila style, with a napkin, a pinch of sugar, a little oil, and a match.

Sometimes, if I had to change platforms, I'd go out to a kiosk and buy a beer for a euro. If not, I just waited. From Potsdamer Platz to at least Nordbahnhof, the journey was disgusting: packed trains.

On the day of my last commute (I was unaware that the gay couple had thrown me out after a jealous quarrel), I managed to get a seat right in the corner of one of the train cars, next to a woman who was talking on her cell phone in an extraterrestrial language, or maybe it was Hungarian. Opposite us were two vacant seats. Or almost vacant: across the narrow space between them lay—very demure, proper, and pretty—a croissant with a single bite taken out of it. At a glance, it looked like a splendid pile of pale shit.

The public outcry against the confection began at Anhalter Bahnhof. Every passenger assumed a jubilant expression on spotting that there were two empty seats ahead, by the door at the end of the car, while so many other people were standing. But then, when they had made their way to sit opposite me and the Hungarian woman talking to a speakerphone voice, they saw the horn-shaped dough that had clearly been in contact with someone's saliva and turned their faces away in disgust, or just stood there staring at the croissant with slightly ridiculous expressions of distaste as they clung to the handrail. After a few moments of referential vacuum, they moved to another part of the car.

The S train was full to the point of overflowing by Potsdamer Platz, as was the indignation inside it. Some passengers exchanged monosyllables (a difficult task in German) or mute glances of reproof: How could anyone in that perfect Lutheran world possibly dare to leave a piece of food on the Other's seat? Were they really unaware that the Great Nightmare consists of unregulated contact with strangers' fluids or the imprint of their fingers? (Unless, of course, it's the Romantic, ecological piss deposited quietly on the grass of the Tiergarten by some invisible fox, or a cuddly, injured wild hedgehog that has to be taken to the vet in a taxi.)

As the train was rounding the tight curve into Friedrichstraße station, I smiled to myself, imagining the fate of that disquieting croissant if it were to find a home on the Mexico City metro. Seventy percent of the passengers would have thrown it onto the floor to take possession of the seat. The remaining 30 percent would have discovered an ingenious way to slip it into their pockets.

I isolated myself from my surroundings with a trick that never fails: letting my eyelids droop like someone dozing, and holding tightly on to my half-empty bottle of Berliner Kindl.

A young couple entered the car. He was handsome and athletic.

She had an extraordinarily beautiful face and was a little overweight. They were both dressed in sportswear and were carrying identical iPods. The young woman talked nonstop in a quiet, slightly frenzied tone. He said nothing. I imagined the reasons for her ill humor: the boyfriend forcing her to go on a diet and lose a few pounds, lectures on self-esteem, jogging in the Mitte during rush hour.

The scene repeated itself: the couple was about to sit down when the bitten croissant (which, by that time, had become a piece of conceptual art in my eyes) made them stop in their tracks. The beautiful, overweight young woman emitted a few little squeaks directed at her boyfriend, as if he'd put the pastry there. But then, when we'd almost reached Oranienburger Straße, with a courage that put to shame the degenerate he-man descendants of inhospitable if extinct barbarian tribes, the woman bent over and, exhibiting a grace that automatically took her down two dress sizes, nudged the croissant with the tip of her iPod into the space between the cushioned seat and the side of the car. She then ordered her partner to sit by the window while she flopped firmly into the aisle seat.

The number of passengers suddenly decreased: the last of those standing got off at Nordbahnhof, and with them the Hungarian woman and her cell phone. The athletic guy kept glancing at the horn-shaped pastry wedged in the gap to the right of his seat (I guessed he was afraid it would return to life from some unknown form of death), while his girlfriend continued to complain about something that was invisible to me. She was still speaking in a quiet voice, but sounded less ill-humored. The train came out of the tunnel and we entered a leafy area. A prerecorded voice announced Nächste station . . .

To my surprise, the chubby girl stood up, kissed her companion quickly on the lips, and got off the S-Bahn at Humboldthain, a station with a deceptively suburban air, surrounded by birch trees. I watched her pass through the door and thought: The guy's a moron. In his shoes, I'd have let her go a little way and then stalked her: the trippy little pig and the big bad wolf. Then I noticed that the athletic young man was watching me watching his girlfriend. It was embarrassing. I let my eyelids droop again and held tightly to my by-then-empty bottle of Berliner Kindl.

By Gesundbrunnen, there was almost no one left in the car. At the other end were an elderly couple, a sour-faced cyclist, and a redheaded woman, but down here only the (ex)boyfriend and I remained. He continued to stare at me. I was still pretending to sleep while spying on him through half-closed lids. The train started up again. Then, as if it were the most natural thing in the world, the guy picked up the bitten croissant and, still looking directly at me, opened his mouth wide, stuck out his long Gene Simmons tongue to give the pastry leisurely licks until it was soaked in saliva. He glanced away from me for a moment to check that none of the other passengers had noticed his actions. This done, he returned his gaze to me and, slipping his hand into his sweatpants, wiped what was left of the croissant across the sweat and bacteria of his balls and groin. Once he'd performed these actions, he rose, put the croissant back between the seats with the diligence of a museographer, and, with a wink to me (that I pretended not to see), left the S-Bahn at Bornholmer Straße.

I continued northward to Pankow and the house belonging to the gay couple, where I found my clothes and my tent thrown into the street. I knocked on the door, knocked again, but as no one answered, I ended up sleeping by the stairs to the U-Bahn.

At least it was spring.

Z

I communicate with my psychoanalyst by phone. My psychoanalyst is called Tadeo. Tadeo pretends to be an impartial judge, but I can see he's in favor of me allowing myself to be bitten. That's no surprise. He was first eaten five months ago.

"It's not a matter of ethics," he says. "It's about solidarity. Which in your case, at an existential level, means continuing to be alone."

I almost burst out laughing: he's talking about existentialism as if he were alive. He's a good National University kid. I change the subject so as not to appear to be making light of his situation.

"Why not come upstairs so we can talk face-to-face? Or at least mouth to ear."

"We are mouth to ear."

"I mean through the door."

"No, my friend," he replies in an extremely somber tone, with the insincere serenity imparted by his academic training. "I've made it a rule not to smell my patients."

"Except for Delfina," I say, hoping to provoke him.

Tadeo clears his throat to cover a brief silence, then responds:

"Delfina has no smell now. And she's not my patient any longer."

For the last year I've been living in the Hotel Majestic, located on one side of the Zócalo in Mexico City. Once a week, Tadeo comes around and does a home psychoanalysis session. At first he used to come up to my room on the fourth floor, we'd make ourselves comfortable (he'd sit on a poorly upholstered chair; I'd perch on the bed) and chat. We generally left the television on to provide some background noise and deaden the carnivorous clacking of the guest in the next room.

Tadeo was the most sensible man I'd ever met until Delfina (I've never seen her, but I imagine she's good-looking) seduced him and, as a sort of tribute, took a few mouthfuls of his left forearm, thus infecting him and causing (without the shadow of a doubt, unintentionally) six months of therapy to go up in smoke. Since then, Tadeo and I have held our sessions via the insipid phone in the lobby.

"Human," I say.

"Pardon?"

"What you mean is that Delfina has no human smell now. Wouldn't it be just the same if you called from your office?"

"Human, yes . . . Honestly, coming here isn't just an overreaction. Who'd connect the call? There's not a soul left in the lobby."

He talks about professionalism, but he was having sex with his clients, eventually fell for one of them, and, because he was in love, allowed himself to be transformed into a beast. Or, not a total beast: a cannibal in transition. I've said this to him, and he acknowledges it, then sadly adds:

"Maybe I should be your patient."

It's a pleasantry. We both know that I'm no good; just a frightened, egotistical master of ceremonies, incapable of helping anyone, even when half the human race is mutating toward death or depression.

Tadeo claims it's not a matter of ethics but solidarity. The truth is that lately it's been a matter of food. I venture out to try to find some after dark. There are hardly any mature somnambulists around at that time: they prefer to hunt during the day, although twilight is their favorite hour.

(There's no reliable data, but it appears that the prolonged ingestion of human flesh eventually leads to—among other things—retinal destruction: bright light is painful, and in the darkness they are like moles. When they go completely blind, they become what I call carnivorous flowers: groaning invalids trailing along the ground. They are still dangerous but strictly sedentary, which makes them relatively simple to avoid.)

In the early days, I was afraid to go outside. I survived on beyond-sell-by-date leftovers from the hotel kitchen: greenish cold cuts, rancid cheese, chocolate, frozen soup, dried fruit . . . However, as the months have passed, I've gained enough confidence not only to make forays to the local stores for provisions but also to have something resembling a social life. My greatest success in that respect has been acting as the emcee of the skateboarding competitions on Eugenia.

My alimentary excursions provide everything I need: from Pachuca empanadas to granola bars, gallon bottles of mineral water to free liquor. The other day, behind the counter of a former print shop, I found a bag of marijuana and another containing what looked like psychotropic pills. I returned them to their place: when it comes to illegal substances, I'm prejudiced.

As long as no one kills me, everything is mine. The country has become a minefield of teeth, but it's also a bargain basement. Thanks to the fantastical efforts of people whose business instincts drive them to do their duty each day, I enjoy a few of the old services that, in some unconscious way, used to make it pleasant to live among humans: fresh Tetra Brik milk in the mornings, for example. A delivery truck still supplies the 7-Eleven on the corner of Moneda and Lic. Verdad, despite the fact that the store has been looted four times in the last week and no one works there anymore: just a few junkie-faced dispatchers with bite marks on their backs who'll take your money as soon as they've ransacked what little remains in the establishment, all the while shaking like ex-boxers with Parkinson's.

A few nights ago I came across an amazing windfall: moldy falafel and hummus, two pounds of pistachios seasoned with garlic and hot chili, half a strip of Coronado Popsicles, a bottle of Appleton Estate rum, and an iPod with—among other vaguely obscure gems—Smetana's "From My Life" . . . I waited until sundown on Friday to celebrate my discovery. I'd decided to have a picnic: headphones on, I took my booty up to the terrace of the Majestic.

When I recount this episode to Tadeo, he falls back on the analytical approach he's been using to treat me for just over a month.

"Have you thought about why you did that?"

"Like I said, to celebrate."

"And you don't think there might be some other reason? Some hidden vein of your need to put yourself in danger? Sunset is the very worst time for you."

I try to change the subject again, but he won't be sidetracked.

"What do you think your neighbors made of it? Did anyone follow you to the terrace?"

"Yeah, one or two of them came to sniff me. Nothing unusual in that. But they did it politely, from a couple of tables away."

With the exception of Lía, a perfectly human Jewish woman who lives on the second floor and whose only activity is foraging for pirated DVDs around the Palacio de Bellas Artes, all the other guests in the Majestic are bicarnal. While they haven't yet come to the point of attacking me, their despairing, glazed expressions—exactly like the ones that used to make crack addicts stand out like sore thumbs—follow me everywhere.

Tadeo refuses to let the topic drop.

"Did they say anything?"

He's beginning to annoy me.

"I wasn't taking much notice of them, because I was spying on the soldiers."

"What soldiers?"

"The ones who come around in the afternoon to take down the flag."

It's the same old routine every day: in the morning, just before sunrise, an armed patrol parades across the Zócalo, unfurling a green, white, and red flag. When it's fully extended, they attach a strong rope and hoist it up a concrete-and-metal pole that's maybe 150 feet high. After that, marching in step with the same panache they displayed on arrival, they leave. The flag, on the other hand, spends the whole day up there, fluttering majestically over thousands of walking corpses and the hundreds of mouths of carnivorous flowers huddled in clumps around the Catedral Metropolitana. In the evening, just before sundown, the soldiers return to collect the gigantic standard: they perform their military ballet in reverse order, detaching and furling the patriotic symbol with exasperating solemnity. Part of their task is to bear the requisite arms. They aren't just for show: almost every day the soldiers find themselves having to carry out the irksome task of executing a couple of the vermin who, having lost whatever brains they ever had, attack the squad without the least respect for their uniforms. In the majority of such cases the soldiers fire at point-blank range, into the temple: the .45-caliber bullets sound dully on the paving stones and the flesh eaters' heads plummet to perform the Last Slam Dance of Mexico City. Even so, the soldiers rarely manage to avoid being nibbled. That might be why more than one of them inevitably stumbles or others attempt to keep their wrists hidden, readjusting the dirty bandages covering their peeling skin.

Practically the whole army has been infected to some extent. There's no telling if this has to do with the constant patrols or the lonely nights in the barracks. And although it's true that they get the best vaccines, it's also the case that cells of deserters spring up on a daily basis (or at least that's what CNN says: the national media have disappeared), at the service of the worm catchers. Anything that still functions here relies on corrupting everything else until it becomes an allegorical mural of destruction.

As happens with any real epidemic, ours began with a few isolated cases, indistinguishable from the general sense of outrage transmitted by the now-defunct (or, depending on how you see it, omnipresent) tabloid press. First, a construction worker murdered his lover and workmate on a building site. The authorities found traces of charred human intestines and heart on a piece of sheet metal placed over hot coals. The accused committed suicide during the trial. A year later, a young poet and professor at the University of Puebla was imprisoned for freezing fragments of his dead girlfriend, which he used as an aid to masturbation. Despite the fact that no one could prove he'd either killed or eaten her, the symptoms this individual displayed in the following years left no room for doubt: he was one of the earliest manifestations of a new reality emerging on the margins, belonging to no kingdom or species. A walking virus.

The first person to come to Mexico to study the phenomenon was an English scientist named Frank Ryan, a virologist whose theory was, in broad outline, that the human species's tremendous evolutionary leap was due not to mammalian DNA but to the high percentage of viral information in our genome. What at first seemed like a polemical hunch capable of explaining diseases like AIDS and cancer became Ryan's Law of Evolution, or the Clinamen of the Species: every organic entropy will eventually lead to the triumph of an entity, neither living nor dead, whose only actions are to feed and reproduce by invading host organisms.

The worst thing about our epidemic, what distinguishes it from every other one, is its annoying slowness. Once an organism has been infected, it displays two defining characteristics: first, the irrepressible urge to feed on human flesh—a desire fueled by smell; second, a gradual multiple sclerosis directly proportional to the quantity of human tissue consumed. It is here that individual willpower affects the process, since the ability to *administer consumption and restructure the appetite* (ridiculous but accurate socioeconomic comparisons employed every day by the Ministry of Health) decides the rate of transformation.

As there is not yet an official list of the evolutionary stages of the organism, in my free time (I have a lot of it) I came up with four categories that I will set out here for the consideration of future carnico-vegetal kingdoms:

The transitioning cannibal is the phase in which my psychoanalyst finds himself. It can last anywhere from a week to a year depending on the individual's medical history, dietary habits, and use of experimental drugs ("Retrovirals and antipsychotics have proved to be helpful," Tadeo said the other day in a tone of academic enthusiasm). In this phase the infected subject loses many vital functions, and so needs little food. The subjects' interaction with their environments is largely unchanged—members of this tribe include the president of Mexico and all his most prominent detractors, leaders of the opposition parties, many doctors and educators, and almost the whole of the business community. The only thing that distinguishes them from someone like me is that they display withdrawal symptoms—nausea, dizziness, hyperventilation—when the smell of real humans is in the air.

The bicarnal creature has reached the stage where it can scarcely resist the temptation to eat you, but, out of a sense of shame, makes its approach with a classic Mexican display of exaggerated good manners: "Would you mind if I accompanied you, sir?" or something similar. This phase is the most revolting of all. I call them bicarnal because, in order to satisfy their appetites, they eat pound after pound of beef, pork, or lamb. They are often found in ruined minimarkets, devouring frozen hamburgers straight from the package. Sitting on the terrace of the Majestic, I once watched a group of them in the center of the Zócalo sacrificing a fighting bull (God only knows where they found it) and then eating the raw flesh. I also call them junkies or worm catchers: their main posthuman activity is trading in corpses. They are the lords and masters of what was once the Historic Center of the capital.

The mature somnambulist walks with a slight hunch and is splattered with the blood of any living thing that has crossed its path. They are blind, feeble, never speak a single word, and, apart from their terrifying appearance, are in fact depressingly dull creatures. They are few in number: this is the shortest stage of the contagion process.

The flower, finally, is the immortal face of what we will all soon be: nascent vegetal man-eaters in a perpetual and pestilential state of putrefaction. As sclerosis overtakes them, mature somnambulists search with what lingering remnant of instinct they possess for a place to drop (un)dead. Although I've occasionally seen solitary carnivorous plants, they are almost always found in clusters, as if the urge toward gregariousness is the last human trait to disappear. I once saw one of those corpses standing upright. But normally they are horizontal, lying in the street or on the floors of their houses, on benches, the roofs of cars, in planters, fountains . . . Rather than actually move, they spasm, and in this way crawl over one another, biting anything that comes within range, including their fellow flowers, constantly opening and closing their jaws (clack, clack, clack, clack, clack), producing a kind of manic teletype sound that used to keep me awake in the early days, and later gave me dreadful nightmares. Now it's a lullaby.

The largest flesh-flower garden in existence grew up around the Catedral Metropolitana, on the side of the Zócalo that the terrace of my hotel overlooks. How could it be otherwise in a Catholic country? Since new terminal cases of the epidemic arrive there around the clock, the amount of food they need also increases. Each morning, buses park in the Zócalo and disgorge groups of devout pilgrims, who pray to God for the salvation of the world and, as proof of their faith, attempt to cross the vegetable patch of teeth that separates them from the doors of the cathedral. Not a single one of them gets even halfway: they are devoured in a matter of minutes, thus keeping the garden well irrigated with blood. It would be the weirdest of tourist attractions if all of Mexico were not already a cemetery.

At the end of our session, Tadeo asks:

"Are you going to come around to do the installation? I'm in Condesa, just off Amsterdam, a block and a half from Insurgentes and Iztaccíhuatl. The nearest metro station is Chilpancingo. I'm on the sixth floor. It's easy to find."

I briefly think it over.

"We don't have to be in the same room," he insists. "We can do it through the intercom."

"It's not you that's the problem. I've just never been that far."

"Come on, man. You'll be fine. I'm on the street every day and nothing happens to me."

"Yes, but you have a car."

"Think of it as a therapeutic exercise in socialization: one way or another, you have to go on living in our world."

He finally convinces me and we agree that I'll come to his home next Monday (today is Friday) to rig up a satellite TV connection.

"But there's one condition," I say. "Forget about doing it over the intercom. I want to see you. I want to see your home. And, of course, I want to see Delfina."

"Why?" he asks suspiciously.

"I dunno . . . To find out what kind of beauty it takes to make a man convert himself into a beefsteak."

Now it's Tadeo who hesitates. But a hundred and forty television channels and fifty music stations, plus ten hard-porn signals and a universal pay-per-view password, all free, is the sort of bribe that no one, not even a cannibalistic Lacanian psychoanalyst, can resist.

"OK," he says, and hangs up.

I consider myself the overlord of this territory, but once, up there in the North, I was master of another: regional maintenance for the largest satellite TV company in the world. For years, I hoarded every imaginable pin, serial number, chip, card, and code in a safe in my desk. I migrated to Mexico City with these tools and toys after the first outbreaks of the epidemic. These small lucky charms represent the multipurpose treasure chest that I sometimes use as coinage: for example, I wager with them in the skateboarders' club on Eugenia, where young punks have invented a version of the old monster truck jumps, this time over rows of the recumbent bodies of cannibalistic flowers. We lay bets on who can jump farthest on his skateboard. The most skillful make it all the way across. The majority return with their calves looking like ground meat due to virus-laden bites.

Things could be worse. Sometimes, in that racetrack of corpses and imbeciles, I win enough for a reinforced rubber and a toothless hooker to suck my dick. And when I'm on a losing streak, I pay my debts by installing a satellite television connection in some residential building in the neighborhood. On a bad day I might have to climb sixty feet above decomposing flesh without a safety harness.

They all want to go on zapping: surfing on a wave of a hundred and forty channels while the love of their life takes slices out of their flesh. All of them. Even the dead ones.

Bring Me the Head of Quentin Tarantino

For Luis Humberto Crosthwaite

I was making coffee when they came for me. Rosendo stood across the street and blew out the door of my house with a bazooka.

(I'm not switching the POV: I saw it all from the window.)

Gildardo made his way through the rubble, went to the kitchen (OK: maybe I am switching the POV), and pointed an AK-47 at me. I was sprawled over the sink, half-deafened, with my face and upper body covered in a dusting of freshly ground Starbucks Sumatra.

"Montaña wants to see you," said Gildardo, grabbing the collar of my pajamas and throwing me onto the freezing tiled floor.

"What about my aunt?" I responded.

My aunt Rosa Gloria Chagoyán lives with me. Or rather, I live in her house. She's eighty-three. While the sicario was dragging me toward the door, I managed to catch a glimpse of her through a smoking hole that the explosion had left in the partition wall. My aunt was in bed, unfazed. She was wearing her yellow terry cloth bathrobe and, as usual, was watching TV with no sound or picture.

Practically on all fours, I passed my bedroom and had a momentary view of the most woeful aspect of the destruction: hundreds of silver disks of my DVD collection littered the floor, and a broken pipe was leaking water onto the metal bookshelves where, until that morning, I'd kept my two thousand porn mags.

"This isn't fair," I said, still being dragged by the collar over the remains of the furniture, the splinters sticking into my ass. "She's a vulnerable old woman."

Outside, Rosendo was stowing the bazooka in the trunk of a Bronco.

"Montaña wants to see you."

"And was it necessary to completely wreck the house for that? A clip on the ear would have done the job, you moron!" I was hysterical.

Rosendo leaned over me with a very stern expression and slapped me hard. I stopped screaming.

They blindfolded me, tied my hands behind my back, and loaded me into what I suppose was the back seat. A couple of minutes passed as they discussed whether I was correctly positioned and if the bonds were tight enough to prevent any attempt to escape.

"Tape his ankles," said one of them.

"Do it yourself," said the other.

Someone passed close to the car.

"Good morning," mumbled Rosendo.

It was my aunt Rosa Gloria Chagoyán, who goes out every morning for bread while I strain the coffee; I recognized the rhythmic clank of her aluminum walker.

"Good morning," Gildardo repeated.

My aunt didn't reply. Good for her.

I heard the click of the car doors locking and then the engine turning over. We crossed Laredo, I guessed heading east. Then, to judge by the steady speed of the Bronco, we got on the Ribereña highway. As far as I could tell, we were making for the Frontera Chica. I passed the time reviewing that morning's events. What I regretted most was having said "to completely wreck the house": split infinitive.

We turned onto a dirt road, the Bronco bucking and swerving. I started feeling nauseated but the motion gradually lulled me into a long, heavy stupor, like a nicotine-induced trance. The SUV came to a stop. They pulled me out, removed the blindfold, and cut the packing tape binding my wrists and ankles. I blinked. Little by little my pupils acclimated to the light. I saw myself barefoot, wearing pajamas, standing in a desert landscape: creosote bushes, yuccas, sweet acacias . . . This had to be Coahuila. My initial instincts had been incorrect; we'd been traveling west the whole time, away from the Frontera Chica. I'm frequently beset by this sort of confusion, and my days in Montaña's territory were no exception. There's an inherent contradiction in my profession: I'm a film critic and the main function of criticism is to misread everything. To imagine it all incorrectly in order to highlight its absurdity.

A few yards from us was an adobe shack, toward which Rosendo pushed me with no concern for the sharp stones cutting into the soles of my feet. Inside the shack was another man, very young, very short, his face covered in tattoos. He was holding a revolver in his left hand and with the right unsuccessfully attempting to tune a portable TV set to some channel.

"Open up," ordered Gildardo.

The kid pressed a switch screwed onto a wooden pole and connected to a long strip of LEDs strung along the back wall. Then he crossed the room and folded up a cot. Underneath was a steel trapdoor with a heavy ring pull. Gildardo propped his AK-47 against the wall.

"Give me a hand."

The tattooed kid once again did as he was told. They grasped the ring and, straining, tugged until they had lifted the hatch. Rosendo pushed me down. Feeling my way blindly, I descended the steep stairway. Rosendo and Gildardo followed. At first the darkness was impenetrable, but once we were four or five yards underground, I began to notice a glow that grew increasingly bright. And a current of fresh air. At the bottom of the stairway I found myself on the mosaic floor of a corridor with a black metal grille at the far end, behind which gleamed an almost natural blue-veined light. The barrier was screened by a couple of climbing plants whose scent I recognized: gardenia and Arabian jasmine. I stopped to breathe in the strange subterranean perfume. Gildardo nudged me forward. As we passed through the gate, I touched one of the plants. The leaves were plastic.

We crossed a polymer garden that smelled of real flora and came to a mahogany door. Rosendo rang a childishly simple code on the bell—two long peals and one short—and we waited. A man opened the door. He was wearing black boxers, a white cotton T-shirt, and, over all that, a yellow terry cloth bathrobe identical to my aunt Rosa Gloria Chagoyán's. He was unshaven, his hair was tangled, and his eyes were red and inflamed, possibly from lack of sleep and the consumption of an incredible amount of whisky on the rocks, a tumbler of which he was holding in his left hand. He looked dirty and smelled of rancid sorghum, but there was something likable, even adorable, about his features despite the protruding jaw visible beneath his beard in the light from the artificial garden.

He looked me in the eyes without blinking or even glancing at my captors.

"Who's this?"

"He was recommended," replied Rosendo warily.

The man in the boxers nodded and allowed us to pass.

During the time it took to enter a cinnamon-colored living room, for the man in the bathrobe to point the remote at a giant plasma screen transmitting a reality show about car chases, for Rosendo to push me toward a sofa and Gildardo to place a bottle of mineral water in my hand, I noted that the bunker was extremely comfortable: spacious, high-ceilinged, airy, with a wide variety of precious objects—ceramics, paintings, bibelots, a Gobelin tapestry—scattered around a suite of what looked like, from the number of doors I could see, five or six rooms. In the background I could hear the whispers and laughter of invisible women, servants, and perhaps children.

The guy in the Rosa Gloria Chagoyán bathrobe stood before me and introduced himself.

"My name is Jacobo Montaña, head of the Sierra Madre cartel, on the lam from the Loma Larga maximum-security prison: the most wanted man in Mexico. Make yourself at home."

Without waiting for me to reply, he pressed a button on the remote for the plasma screen and asked:

"Do you know who this is?"

I recognized the scene: it was from the final sequence of *Django Unchained,* when the protagonist manages to escape from his enforced journey to the mines and returns to Candie's plantation to exact revenge. The editing shows a complete lack of taste. Quentin Tarantino appears on the screen (a little plumper than usual in his cowboy costume) and, when he's in midsentence, the dynamite that is strapped to his torso explodes, blowing him to smithereens.

Montaña paused the movie.

"Are you familiar with him?"

"Naturally."

"Have you met him in person?"

I was about to laugh, but Montaña's seriousness stopped me in my tracks. I shook my head.

"I wrote my master's thesis on his work."

"But you know where he lives, right?"

"Not precisely. Or, well, yes, in L.A., but . . ."

Montaña turned to Rosendo and Gildardo. He cracked his knuckles.

"You heard him, bloodhounds: you're going to L.A. Bring me the head of that fucking bastard. Ask Dante for funds. He'll give you whatever you need."

"Yes, sir."

Rosendo and Gildardo retraced their steps to the grille.

"And what about me?" I screeched in panic.

"You stay here with me, champ," said Montaña with nauseating obsequiousness: he sat down beside me and put an arm around my shoulders. "You're going to teach me everything there is to know about that sonofabitch."

With his face close to mine, when I could make out, beneath the hair and in the depths of his blurry eyes, the weariness and fury of his voluntary imprisonment (I didn't know it at the time, but that specter had spent fifteen months coordinating the largest narcotics operation in the history of the world from his underground residence), I realized why Jacobo Montaña had seemed so handsome to me: his features were identical to those of the man whose decapitation he had just ordered. His face was the face of Quentin Tarantino.

—

The title of my master's thesis is "Parody and the Sublime: The Character Overhears Himself in the Work of Quentin Tarantino." Thanks to that document, I was awarded a couple of academic prizes, gained a certain level of celebrity among low-life geeks, and was offered paid employment: writing a column on cinema, published three times a week in a dozen newspapers. That, on top of the modest fortune I administer in the name of my aunt Rosa Gloria Chagoyán, allowed me to return from what used to be known as D.F. and is now CDMX to a comfortable life in Laredo.

(I'm sorry, I can't stand Chilangos, I detest them, there's no getting away from it: they might be cosmopolitan when considered as a whole, but block by block they are more provincial and class-conscious than I am.)

What is meant by parody and by the sublime? There is an unforgettable text that addresses the latter: the brief treatise *On the Sublime* by Pseudo-Longinus (that is to say, by an unknown author whom we now recognize by that attribution), written sometime in the first century BCE. The epistle—Greek in the original—speaks of "heights," "grandeur," "elevation"; voices that coincide with what in Latin is called *sublimis*: raised from the ground or suspended in the air. From that it can be inferred that the art of the sublime is that realm in which beauty, grandeur, and profundity reign. It is, nevertheless, of utmost importance not to confuse elevation with haughtiness, pedantry, or solemnity. From the first pages of his work, Pseudo-Longinus himself warns that there are pretentious forms that cloud, or "sully," Beauty. He instructs us against "swelling" (a commonplace in cinema; cases in point: the works of Michael Bay and Mel Gibson), a vice that results in grandiloquence rather than heightening. He also suggests that artists should avoid puerility at all costs (all Mexican cinema seems puerile to me, but in my thesis I illustrate this point with reference to Carlos Reygadas): "Men slip into this kind of error because, while they aim at the uncommon and elaborate and most of all at the attractive, they drift unawares into the tawdry and affected." Pseudo-Longinus then speaks of "mad enthusiasm" (an "unseasonable and empty passion," which reminds me of Roland Emmerich) and "frigidity"—something Lars Von Trier and the whole Dogme #95 movement fall victim to at their worst—and of authors who "sometimes forget themselves for the sake of such paltry pleasantries."

Yet, in my judgment, the most interesting thing about the short text *On the Sublime* is not the skill with which it informs us about the rhetorical traps that chip away at greatness but its emphasis on the notion that profound beauty, the beauty that truly moves us, arises not from natural conditions (that is, from the individual genius of each author) but from the systematic daily practice of technique that is the basis of all aesthetic work. According to this precept, the sublime is learned; it is not epiphany, much less entelechy. This notion, which is clearly common sense, contradicts almost the entire history of Western art.

Let me put it another way. In the second paragraph of his work, Pseudo-Longinus states:

> First of all, we must raise the question whether there is such a thing as an art of the sublime or lofty. Some hold that those are entirely in error who would bring such matters under the precepts of art. A lofty tone, says one, is innate, and does not come by teaching; nature is the only art that can compass it. Works of nature are, they think, made worse and altogether feebler when wizened by the rules of art. But I maintain that this will be found to be otherwise if it be observed that, while nature as a rule is free and independent in matters of passion and elevation, yet is she wont not to act at random and utterly without

> system. Further, nature is the original and vital underlying principle in all cases, but system can define limits and fitting seasons, and can also contribute the safest rules for use and practice.

What Pseudo-Longinus is explaining, pace Rilke, is that *not every angel is terrifying.* From his POV, Beauty is not simply that state of terror that calmly disdains to destroy us. Beauty, he thinks, cannot be an irrational force of Nature; rather, it is Nature in a classical and harmonious state: a periodic table, something humans are capable of studying and learning. Is that opinion important for our spiritual conception of art? It is extremely important. To begin with, because it posits the existence of tradition, that is to say, of a cultural genealogy: every present aesthetic object carries the metaphorical genes (and memes) of an aesthetic object that existed in the past. Every text is the result of an *architext* (as Gérard Genette calls it; and as I feel about it as I write this story and think, for example, about how deeply I have been influenced by Hermann Broch—and how few of his books have ever been sold). Nothing is original, originality is an illusion: each and every narrative—however much it might appeal to us or move us—has its origins in an earlier one. And that narrative comes from another, and so on, at least until Homer. This is to say—and I return to Genette here—that every narrative is, in the etymological sense, a *parody,* a *parallel ode.*

If the sublime is an aesthetic value that is not a gift of Nature but something that must be learned through technique, then the only plausible means of producing sublime art is by producing parodies. Parody is the sublime. The sublime is parody. Except that most of us believe that the sacred exists and that, as Pedro Almodóvar said in an interview, "technique is an illusion." Even atheists (I'm an atheist) know that language is sacred. If you don't believe me, take a lit cigarette and a picture of your daughter and burn the eyes out.

This is where Greek and contemporary treatise writers go down the drain, where the only thing left to tie us to the world is the irrationality of parody and the sublime. To give one example: Barry

White's voice when he sings "Can't Get Enough of Your Love, Babe." No one believes that voice to be true. But we all know that it's the voice of Truth.

—

A Barry White song is playing: "Can't Get Enough of Your Love, Babe." It's midafternoon. An olive-green two-door Maverick '74 is heading west along an empty desert highway. It passes a sign reading "Bernal NMex."

"Twenty-five miles," says Gildardo grouchily from the driver's seat.

"Stop complaining, just drive," replies Rosendo, who is sitting in the passenger seat, attempting to match his words to the rhythm of the song while moving his torso in some graceless form of dance.

Both men are wearing dark glasses to protect their eyes from the strong direct sunlight.

"A twenty-fucking-five-mile detour to Bernal," repeats Gildardo.

Rosendo ignores him and continues gyrating to Barry White.

"And another twenty-five back to Route 66. Fifty miles there and back."

"Take it easy, man. When you get a taste of the pizzas and the mezcal, you're gonna say, 'Oh my gosh,' like the bitch you are."

Gildardo drives in silence for a few seconds then asks:

"Who recommended it?"

"My cousin Matías, the hired gun. He used to guard shipments of Oaxaca crystal traveling from Pinotepa to Piedras Negras on 57 Norte. Down there in Oaxaca he got a taste for mezcal and discovered this shit: *paplometl* distilled in clay pots. Fifty-four percent alcohol. Every shot with more of a kick than three lines."

"And then?"

"And then what?"

"Wasn't there a broad in the picture?"

"You're a horny bastard. There was a broad. A black-haired woman by the name of Silvana. She was going with my cousin but then she left him for a chef called Renato. He makes the pizzas."

"Well, your cousin's a moron. If a chick left me for some Italian fairy, they'd both feel my Magnum where the sun don't shine."

"Argentinian."

"What?"

"Renato is Argentinian."

"Square dick in a round hole."

"Matías says he liked the kid and they ended up buddies. Then Renato got in deep shit with the immigration dudes and my cousin helped him to come north and open a pizzeria. Silvana shuttles back and forth from Oaxaca with the mezcal. There's no shortage. Mezcal and pizza, dude: it's the future. To hell with the frigging cargos of crystal and blow."

It's sundown. The Maverick enters a small town. Gildardo parks in front of a bar with an unlit neon sign that says "Pinotepa Nacional" and "mezcal&pizza." Rosendo gets out of the car. In one hand he holds an iPod Classic, in the other a portable speaker from which comes the voice of Barry White, now singing "Never Gonna Give You Up."

Gildardo turns off the ignition, gets out, locks the doors, and looks around. Opposite the bar is a billboard that announces: "Welcome to Bernal, Land of Friendship."

"Goddamn Bernal," says Gildardo.

They go into the pizzeria. It's extremely small: two tables and a counter. At the back is a barely visible kitchen area and a piece of cardboard with an arrow drawn in crayon pointing to the left and, under the arrow, also written in crayon, the letters "W.C."

A gringo-gringo just over thirty with the swaggering air of an overgrown teenage ranchero welcomes them from behind the counter.

"Hello, folks!"

Rosendo puts his iPod Classic and the speaker on one of the two tables. "Never Gonna Give You Up" is still playing.

"Are you Renato?" asks Rosendo.

"Nope," replies Gringo-Gringo.

"Do you speak Spanish?" asks Gildardo.

"Nope," replies Gringo-Gringo. "But if you want, I can make you a pizza," he continues in English. "Piz-za," he repeats in an overdone Italian accent. "*The Sopranos*, know what I mean?"

Gildardo flops into one of the chairs, doubled over with laughter. Rosendo sits down opposite his partner. He seems disconcerted.

"So?" asks Gringo-Gringo. "To pizza or not to pizza?"

Rosendo nods. Gringo-Gringo moves to the kitchen. Still laughing, Gildardo says:

"Twenty-five miles. And twenty-five back to the natural route. I'll tell you something, dude. Seems to me this is something I knew, then forgot, and just remembered again."

Rosendo steps up to the counter. On the other side, behind a curtain, Gringo-Gringo can be seen preparing the pizza dough, rolling it out on a board.

"And the Argentinian? And his Mexican woman?" Rosendo asks.

"Don't know nothing about no Argentinians," replies Gringo-Gringo. "I might have seen someone with a big nose but I can't say if he was Italian or Jewish. I did see the woman: she transferred the business to me. I don't think she was Mexican. Too cute an ass to be Mexican, and she had no belly. I'd say she was Indian. Maybe Navajo or Puebla."

"Oaxaqueña."

"Could be. To my way of thinking, those people don't have a race, you know. They're all stray dogs."

Rosendo returns to his seat. Gildardo attempts to stifle a fresh burst of laughter. Gringo-Gringo comes out from behind the curtain and asks:

"Something to drink?"

Looking nowhere in particular, Rosendo suggests:

"Mezcal."

"Never heard of it. I've got Corona and Tecate."

"Two Tecates," says Gildardo.

Gringo-Gringo moves away, but Rosendo insists:

"*Aguardiente*? Snake bite? Didn't the last owners leave a single bottle?"

Gringo-Gringo comes back to the table with a disapproving expression.

"I might have three or four bottles of that colorless, no-label shit in the cupboard. Can't think why a white man would risk drinking it, not even a white Mexican. But I'll fetch some for you if that's what you want."

Night has fallen. The portable speaker and the iPod are still playing quietly: now it's "I've Got So Much to Give." Rosendo and Gildardo look halfway drunk. They glance at each other, cackle: it's as if the world is orbiting around them. They clink *veladora* glasses brimming with mezcal and make a toast.

"*Papalometl* agave, pop," says Rosendo. "Distilled in clay pots. Fifty-four percent alcohol. You won't find liquor this good anywhere in the American South or northern Mexico."

On the table are the remains (in fact, almost all) of a disgustingly greasy-looking deep-dish pizza.

Rosendo gets to his feet, hugs Gildardo, kisses him on the forehead, makes to clink glasses once more, and observes:

"If I was your cousin, I'd have killed her. Even if she was real hot and had a cute name. If a woman left me for some Italian fairy, I'd fucking kill her."

"Argentinian," replies Rosendo. "Renato is Argentinian."

"*Salud*," says Gildardo. "Here's to life."

Gringo-Gringo comes out of the kitchen, stands in front of his clients, arms akimbo, and, with a broad, self-satisfied grin, says:

"My dad punched Barry White."

Rosendo and Gildardo look at each other in silence. Gringo-Gringo moves closer and, still speaking, slaps their shoulders and backs.

"Don't get me wrong: there's nothing racist about it. I mean to say: Barry White was a fucking fat Negro. We can all agree that Barry White was a fucking fat Negro, right? But that's not the point. To begin with, it was the seventies. Wow: were they hard times. I wasn't even born. Everyone was stoned out of their minds, sometimes on three or four different drugs at once. But not Dad: Dad was a very sensible young man. He always told us: beer and nothing more. And he practiced what he preached.

"Dad would have been . . . what? Twenty-four, twenty-five? He'd always wanted to be a good family man. You know how it is, right? Either you have principles or you let the train flatten you.

"He went to Albuquerque looking for work. Those were dark times. Not just for you Mexicans, and that's all I have to say: we real Americans have had our dose of suffering, too, since you guys, excuse my language, have become such whiners. I mean no offense, just saying it like it is. So there's my dad: a pure white in Albuquerque in the midseventies. And what did they give him? A crummy job as a bellboy in the Brighton Hotel, a small old building in the Sandia Valley. At least it had some class. After only a few days my poor dad had a chance to show what he was worth: Barry White arrived for some gala event he was doing that night.

"Dad says it was one of the high points of his life, watching that big man with his little hat checking in, and then he had the joy of carrying his luggage to his room (he says that while they were going up in the elevator, Barry White was breathing real heavy, like someone kept sticking their finger up his ass), and watching him dry his fucking fat Negro sweat on a white towel.

"But the trouble started early the next morning. Barry came back from his gig really drunk, lit up, probably high on drugs. First he hit the cab driver who'd brought him back—he didn't want to pay—then he shouted all sorts of shit at the reception clerk and, without so much as an apology, made for the elevators, where Dad was waiting for him in the dumb page boy outfit and white gloves they used to wear back then.

"'Fucking Negro,' Dad said he was thinking. 'He'd better not touch me.'

"He was terrified: Barry White was a real giant of a man."

The iPod and the speaker play Barry White singing a version of "Just the Way You Are."

"Dad pressed the button for the fourth floor. On the way, Barry

White smiled at him. So far so good. When the elevator stopped, Barry exited through the folding door and took out his billfold to give Dad a tip. My dad says that he seemed to him such a fucking lousy fat, drunk Negro that, without giving it a second thought, he punched him on the nose, knocking his ass to the carpet. Just to teach him some respect. My poor dad paid for that light-bulb moment with three months in the can."

Rosendo and Gildardo look each other in the eyes. There's an overlong silence; the only sound is the music from the iPod. Then, as if they have come to an agreement, they throw themselves on Gringo-Gringo. Rosendo gets his right arm around his neck and covers his mouth with his left hand. Gildardo punches him in the gut and pushes him toward the kitchen. They crash into the counter and then the stove. Gildardo holds Gringo-Gringo's face over one of the burners and lights the gas. He pulls his hand away from the flame, grabs a frying pan hanging on the wall, positions it over one side of Gringo-Gringo's face, and uses it to force his head onto the flames. Gringo-Gringo howls and twitches, simultaneously begs forgiveness and curses in some unintelligible language. Rosendo pulls one of Gringo-Gringo's arms toward the kitchen table, takes the wooden rolling pin Gringo-Gringo had used to stretch the pizza dough, and repeatedly brings it down on the bones of his hand and wrist. The two men assault and torture their victim for an indeterminate length of time; they cut him with a kitchen knife, pour salt on the open wounds, smash his elbows and kneecaps . . .

Rosendo and Gildardo finally loosen their hold on Gringo-Gringo and his body falls to the floor: he's bleeding, his face is burned, and several of his bones are broken. His breathing comes in gasps. Rosendo and Gildardo extract identical .357 Magnums from their holsters and empty their cylinders into the defenseless body, without rage, almost playfully.

It's dark and the street is mostly in shadows: the only illumination comes from the windows of shops and the few nearby houses.

Gildardo is sitting in the driver's seat of the Maverick '74. The engine is running.

"Fifty fucking miles there and back," he mutters.

Inside the vehicle, Barry White is still singing.

Rosendo comes out of the Pinotepa Nacional mezcal&pizza restaurant, whose neon sign is now lit. Smoking a cigarette, he looks to the left and right; the street is silent, empty. His gaze falls on the sign across the street: "Welcome to Bernal, Land of Friendship."

"Goddamn Bernal," he says.

He throws his cigarette butt to the ground and gets into the car through the front passenger door. The Maverick pulls out and disappears into the New Mexico desert night.

Perhaps I should narrate my kidnapping as if it were a film script, concentrating on the visuals, sparing myself having to bankroll the unpopularity that comes with reflection. But the thing is that I don't make movies; I'm just a critic, and that's my POV. And if Jacobo Montaña hadn't looked identical to Quentin Tarantino and hadn't later agreed—from jail—to do the interview that might help explain his strange obsession with decapitating his double, my story would be incapable of inspiring even a shred of morbid interest.

My writing and the classes I've taught on Q always focus on two issues that have nothing to do with technique or even narratology: the axiological question and the Shakespearian nature of the characters. I'm convinced that the depth of his work doesn't depend simply on the mise-en-scène and the management of temporal elements (two rubrics celebrated by half the human race), but above all on the invention of sublime characters, something that Harold Bloom related to the tension between cognitive power and tragedy.

Q's characters inhabit a universe of *disordered ethical states.* And in this they are not dissimilar to those of the great English-language dramatists, from Marlowe and Shakespeare to Sam Shepard and Harold Pinter. Any attempt to subsume the creations of these writers under the precepts of realism would be inappropriate: their ethic is purer, their pragmatism has less to do with profit and loss than with attachment to the present in terms of revelation; a sense of the present not as reality but as yearning, something perpetually on the verge of happening; they are Macbethian entities. Whether it's Jules Winnfield and his exposition on the miracle of the bullets, Vincent Vega in front of the mirror convincing himself not to fuck Mia Wallace (because *it's a matter of principle*), Beatrix Kiddo, who at every stage of her vengeance discovers that hatred is the most mature state of love, or Standartenführer Hans Landa, who uses charisma as a tool of psychological terror, Q's characters are faithful to an epileptic ethics. Honesty, solidarity, discipline, and loyalty are their driving forces, the fuel that has converted them into killing machines. It's a code of cruelty, not blind cruelty, that makes Lt. Aldo Raine brand Hans Landa's forehead at the end of his peregrination, and similar scruples cause Butch to return for his father's gold watch, bear Fabienne's teasing with patience, pull a fast one on Marsellus Wallace, and be indifferent (or at least seem indifferent) to the death of Floyd, his rival in the boxing ring. The primitive family is the basis of Butch's ethical code (although the character is also panicked by the prospect of fatherhood, as can be inferred from his erotic dialogue with Fabienne, in the sense that he'd kick her in the belly if she started one, and prefers oral to genital sex), and almost anything outside that order can go to hell—except for violent sodomy, the ultimate negation of family values: that is, of reproduction. This is perhaps why Bruce Willis's avatar rescues Marsellus Wallace—another family man—when he is being fucked in the ass, that temple of time where, for years, both Butch's father and Christopher Walken keep the gold watch that represents the boxer's right to be born. From my POV, it isn't pity or decency that drives him as he searches for a samurai sword in the stock of the hock shop: it's his adherence to the hetero-patriarchal code. Protecting the manhood of another male, even if he's your enemy, guarantees the continued existence of our species, and related to that is a strange double-sided allegory in which the character becomes a representation of his own father raised from the dead; Marsellus Wallace substitutes Captain Koons; Zed and Maynard embody a psychotic version of the Vietcong, and the samurai sword rises up as a redemptive oxymoron of the gold watch. It is a complex web of moral symbols because Tarantino is a born moralist.

I tried to explain all this to Jacobo Montaña but he became impatient and threatened to kill me. I had to find other, less irritating ways to entertain him. It wasn't unusual for him to lose his cool, insult me, break things. Nevertheless, I want to be clear that he never physically mistreated me during the twelve days of my abduction. On the contrary, he made sure that every comfort his home offered was available to me: "Whatever you need, champ," he was in the habit of saying, like someone trying to please a child. Whatever I needed included steam baths, a gymnasium (that I never used), a luxurious bedroom, international cuisine, designer clothing, several pairs of shoes, satellite channels, and the favors of two young prostitutes, whom I ordered from a catalog and who were available twenty-four hours a day in the week before my rescue. Whenever I mention this, the public accuses me of suffering from Stockholm syndrome. I don't find that judgment unfair: after all, it's a rare privilege to be kidnapped by the evil twin of your favorite movie director.

We watched everything he had on hand. Not just the *Reservoir Dogs / The Hateful Eight* cycle, but the shorts, the minor collaborative pieces, other people's work based on Q's screenplays, and some throwaways for television. We visited the obvious sources with the intention of digesting these references before returning to the canonical corpus: *City on Fire, Django, Once Upon a Time in the West, Game of Death* (any excuse to go back to the great Bruce Lee), *Unforgiven, The Good, the Bad and the Ugly* . . . I was careful to avoid the work of challenging directors like Godard, Hitchcock, and Kurosawa, although we did watch and enjoy *Seven Samurai, Band of Outsiders,* and *Vertigo.*

Montaña hates anything pretentious, but he has a gift for spotting the nuances in a simple story. Even though he has watched a great deal of cinema, his frame of reference is basic. Among his favorites are *Mackenna's Gold*, almost any classic Western, the two *Scarface* movies, *Heat*, *Die Hard*, *Lethal Weapon*, *Under Siege*, and anything with Dolph Lundgren or Van Damme. Plus *El tunco Maclovio* and the whole of Mario Almada's catalog.

He always hated it when Quentin Tarantino appeared on-screen. During his scenes, Montaña would pretend to be busy with something else: filing his nails or making a sandwich in the kitchen. It was as though he loathed his own image in the hyperviolent mirror of parody.

"Why do you want to kill him?" I asked.

"Because he rubs me the wrong way."

This was said in such a sinister tone that I never mentioned it again during the time we spent together in the bunker.

The movies, like everything else, came to us via Dante Mamulique, the administrator of Montaña's patrimony. Contemporary artworks, antique furniture, kitsch armchairs bought in Galerías El Triunfo, fashionable attire that Jacobo treated like kitchen rags, electronic gadgetry, collectible toys, video games and consoles, jewelry designed by Teresa Margolles based on objects that had once belonged to my host's victims: Dante Mamulique was a sort of Oscar Wilde, who (to fill life with beauty) sent bulging envelopes to a person who could not appreciate their contents; an unrepentant heir to Dostoevsky and *Notes from Underground*.

"The moron brought me a smartphone with an app for catching Pokémons. It's clear as day he's never lived thirty feet beneath the earth's surface."

Life in the bunker was pleasant but dreary. We had more than enough of everything, yet had lost the illusion of freedom. It's not like I went out much when I was living in Aunt Rosa Gloria Chagoyán's house: I used to order everything I needed online, and other than during breakfast, or when my aunt asked me to rub Fresca Pie into the backs of her knees, or the weekly day trip over to the other side to watch all the new releases in the multiplexes, I spent long hours in my room. The bunker, as I said, was more comfortable and full of amenities. But I missed the fiction of *going out*, and without fiction, human beings are like Olympic swimming pools with no water.

As the days passed, I got to know some of the security team and the two wives who accompanied Montaña in his ascetic life: silent people accustomed to obeying orders. I still believe there were children living there, despite the fact that they were never visible; I used to hear them in the distance in the late afternoon, possibly playing baseball or Nintendo. I also met a couple of suppliers, who brought news from the surface. Up there, they were killing one another with such brutality that it didn't seem like such a bad idea to live forever in that fortress filled with the garden-scented plastic flowering plants that—at moments of peak lunacy—Jacobo used to water. In Laredo, Reynosa, and the Frontera Chica there were daily shootouts. The army and the federal police had occupied a luxury hotel in my hometown, turning it into a sort of barracks. Each and every member of the municipal police force had been arrested, charged with corruption and crimes against public health. And in Coahuila, a few minutes' drive from our subterranean prison, they had just found a mass grave in which, it was said, half the inhabitants of a small town lay reduced to ashes.

I never associated that violence with my captor's business activities. That may have been due to the aforementioned Stockholm syndrome, but it's possible there's a simpler, more egotistical reason. As the days went by, Jacobo turned into a disciple, at times an awkward one, but a disciple nonetheless: he attempted to follow my cinematic reflections on this or that scene, asked pertinent questions with an eagerness to hear the answer that none of my other students had ever displayed, was capable of sitting through three or even four movies without a break, and, finally, treated me with extreme deference in everything related to the seventh art. His enthusiasm, combined with the perfect portrait of Quentin Tarantino that was his face (when I asked him to shave and comb his hair, he consented; he had a barber brought in from Piedras Negras), prevented me from seeing him as a criminal. For me, Jacobo Montaña was an obscene mix of master and pupil. Likability is one of the most insidious packages of Evil.

I discovered that the bunker was much larger than I'd first imagined; in another era or a different place it could well have accommodated a small military complex. In addition to the main house and garden, there were storerooms, passages, unused games areas (for example, a small basketball court with just one hoop, but equipped with an electronic scoreboard, two rows of bleachers, and a floodlight), classrooms, and meeting rooms . . . After my third day in captivity, Montaña allowed me to take a solitary evening stroll through the underground world. "It's not like you're gonna escape," he said with a laugh, by way of a warning.

I explored as much of our walled city as was possible. I don't believe I saw everything: its tentacles extended beyond the Río Bravo, and I may even, at some point, have inadvertently crossed beneath the ground and water, from Mexico to the United States. In their confused plotting, those strolls represented the area of fiction that saved me from despair. Those, and cinema. Now that I come to think of it, cinema must be the art form that has the most in common with being confined in an ant colony thirty feet belowground.

It's five in the afternoon, Venice Beach, California. Rosendo is sauntering along one of the walkways running parallel to the water. He's carrying a supermarket bag. The scenic route abounds with dogs and their owners, roller skaters, skimpily clad people, "loverboys," and vendors of medical marijuana. Rosendo enters a seafront motel. He opens the door to a room. Inside, on a king-size bed, is Gildardo. He has taken off his shirt. Between grimaces of pain, he's carefully attempting to clean an open wound in his right armpit.

"This is all I could find," says Rosendo grouchily, throwing the plastic bag at his colleague's feet.

Gildardo leans over and inspects the contents: a bottle of Wild Turkey, a large packet of cotton balls, a bottle of peroxide, and a couple of comics.

Rosendo flops onto the other side of the bed. In the background a Norteño song plays softly:

I've got bad feelings
in my heart.
It's just I can't
afford your prices.
Don't try me, babe
I'm playing straight.
Don't force me to say
what I really think.
I've got bad feelings,
and it's not from anger:
pain is prettier than rage.
What sadness leaves,
and you know it,
is the taste of the desert
in every place.
I've got bad feelings,
but they're against myself:
you're leaving me
because I'm playing it cool,
because the fire of my love
isn't strong enough
to swim upriver
through your love.
I've got bad feelings in my guts
because it's not promises
that deceive but the illusions
no one offered you.
Love is giving
what you don't have
to someone who doesn't want it,
and that was the story
between you and me.

Gildardo opens the Wild Turkey and takes a swig from the neck. He goes on patiently treating his wound as they speak.

"So, you gonna keep up that sour mood? It ain't my fault I saved your life."

Rosendo glances at his wristwatch. He stands up.

"Forget saving my life. Just don't ever again take me anywhere that crazy cokehead bitch suggests."

"A job's a job. If you wanna find Quintintino, you gotta go to every party in Hollywood, that's what they say."

"Yeah, Gildardo, but that wasn't Hollywood. Melanie's taking you for a ride. She goes on giving you tip-offs so you'll buy her soda. And Mamulique's funds aren't going to last forever."

"We ask for more."

"Then Montaña's gonna want to know what the fuck we're doing with his money."

"We're following his orders."

"We're living it up, knucklehead. Parties, drugs, and women in L.A. Every day we get more like those soft dudes we're always bad-mouthing."

"Speak for yourself, asshole. You didn't just get a knife stuck in your armpit."

"They're gonna kill us. For insubordination."

"Only if we lose the thread. A job's a job, and this time we got a sweet one. Take it from me, we'll flush out Quintintino."

"They all talk a lot, but it's months since anyone saw him."

"They've seen him, they just haven't said where. No one goes and vanishes for months at a time. Not even if the moron's name is Jacobo Montaña."

"You'll believe anything anyone tells you! What makes you think an actor's going to turn up at a dogfight like that one last night?"

"He's not an actor. Or at least, the boss hates him because he's sometimes an actor, but that's not all Quintintino is."

"Square dick in a round hole. We were lucky to get out alive."

"Because I saw them first, dude. If it hadn't been for me, that bonerdome bastard would have had your guts on the floor. I'm still waiting for the thank-you card."

"And you wouldn't have a hole in your armpit if we'd steered clear of the sort of crummy dives Tarantino's never going to show his face in. Forget about Melanie and let's find another source."

"What d'you mean, 'Forget about Melanie,' you knucklehead? You've seen the boobs on her. If you want another source, go find it yourself."

There's a knock on the door. Rosendo takes his gun from a drawer in the desk and sneaks a look out of the window. When he sees that the person knocking is young, good-looking, and blonde, he rolls his eyes. He lowers the gun and opens the door.

"*Quihubo*, Melanie?"

"Hi, Ros," she replies without looking at him.

Melanie enters the room, closing the door behind her. She throws herself onto Gildardo, who is still cleaning his armpit.

"For god's sake," Gildardo says, wincing. "Wait, can't you?"

Melanie rolls off Gildardo and, with an offended pout, retreats to one corner of the room. She picks up the bottle of Wild Turkey and takes a swig.

"You got anything?"

"Have you?" asks Rosendo.

Melanie ignores him. Gildardo rummages in the desk drawer at his side and extracts a small bag of cocaine. He hands it to Melanie, who takes a couple of snorts from the nail of her little finger.

"I think today's the day, guys. DJ Daredevil is in town from New York, and my friend Lissie told me Q never misses one of his gigs. This is our lucky night."

"You've been saying that for four fucking days, Mel," says Rosendo as he returns the Magnum to the drawer.

Melanie perches on one of Gildardo's thighs and unbuttons her blouse.

"This is L.A., sweetheart. If you want something, anything, you gotta be a party goblin."

Gildardo kisses the nape of her neck.

"You wanna play?" asks Melanie. She takes off her blouse without removing her eyes from Rosendo for a moment.

Rosendo leaves the room.

Outside, the sun is dipping in the sky. Rosendo crosses the parking lot and walks on toward the beach. As he does, he takes a cell phone from the pocket of his jacket and dials a number. He waits. The phone rings a couple of times.

"Yes?" says a woman's voice at the other end of the line.

"Estrellita," Rosendo croons. "I've been wanting to call you so badly."

"Rosendo, my love. How are you? I knew it was you."

Estrellita—the woman on the other end of the line—is sitting in a wheelchair in the middle of an empty room. She's around seventy and, judging by the milky whiteness of her eyes, is blind. Her apartment is in shadows. Behind her, rays of strong artificial light enter through the window.

"Where are you, Rosendo, my dear?"

Rosendo has reached the boardwalk by the beach.

"You're not going to believe this: I'm in Los Angeles, California. I never imagined my job would take me so far."

"Holy Mary, Mother of God. I hope you don't come across too many of those movie actresses. They say they haven't an ounce of shame. Give you the Judas kiss as soon as look at you."

"Don't worry yourself, Estrellita: not a single one of them has come my way. I'm in a very pretty place called Venice Beach. Shall we get started?"

"Just wait one second."

Estrellita puts her cordless phone in her lap and wheels herself into the artificial light entering through the window. Once she arrives and is bathed in the external glow, she picks up the instrument again.

"There. Whenever you're ready."

"I'm walking along a wooden path: a boardwalk, they call it. The wood is the color of dark coffee, and very springy, like it was freshly cut and still moist. Two blond gringo guys in sleeveless T-shirts are coming toward me. They're drinking beer, a brand that looks like small Caguamas, in brown paper bags. Their skin's badly burned from so much time in the sun."

"Wretches. Drinking in the street."

"It's the beach, Estrellita."

"Ah."

"Ahead of me there's a girl with a dog. I don't know what breed, but it's real cute, long red hair. Jittery; it's prancing about like it wants to run off."

"A golden retriever, it has to be."

"Yeah, I think so."

"But, no, you said red hair, right?"

"Yeah, red."

"Then it must be an Irish Setter."

"You've got it, Estrellita. You should see how pretty it looks with the sun reflecting off its coat."

"But isn't it nighttime?"

"Not here, not yet. The sun's only just going down. It's two hours earlier in Los Angeles, Estrellita."

"Heavens above."

"Do you want me to describe the beach for you?"

"Oh, yes, please, go ahead."

Rosendo gives her a detailed description of the sea, the sand, and what's going on in Venice Beach. On the other end of the line his voice gradually disappears into the empty eyes of the elderly woman.

I know of two opposing views related to the notion that parody and the sublime are complementary, even at times interchangeable, aesthetic concepts. The first of these is the work of the novelist Hermann Broch. The second is a general theory of literature devised by Professor Harold Bloom.

José María Pérez Gay says that Broch's first creation—dating from 1908, when the Viennese author was only twenty-two years old—was "a machine for blending textile fibers" that Hermann co-patented with the head of the local business school where he was a student. Broch was a prodigy who started writing late in life, in part because he dedicated his youth to being the relatively effective heir to his father's textile mill, but also because of the philosophical complexity of his style. I'd like to underscore this irony (or if I allow myself to fall into excess, this parody—the unconscious is outside): the author's first invention was "a machine for blending text(ile) materials," and I will now abandon the industrial metaphor.

The context for Broch's writing is the twilight of the Austro-Hungarian aspiration to classical status, an incarnation of Western thought that Pérez Gay analyzes in *El imperio perdido*. The Austro-Hungarian Empire is to neoliberal thought what the Soviet Union is to Marxism-Leninism, and I'm surprised that the twenty-first century should have so little curiosity about the former of those two cultural failures. Not in historical or political terms, but simply as tragedy.

In the early twentieth century, Germanic novelistic thought was—like Proust's and Joyce's—deeply concerned with the problem of the sublime. But in contrast to Thomas Mann, whose discourse always displayed an element of paradox, the Austrians Robert Musil and Hermann Broch attempted an impossible flight—a fugue in the musical sense: to rewrite the *architext*; not to generate a pristine narrative event, without genealogy. This attempt—at once guttural and aristocratic—to return to origins and renounce parody (that is to say, tradition) is evident in Musil's *The Man without Qualities* and Broch's most celebrated narrative trilogy, *The Sleepwalkers*. But it is also an impulse that appears in "Worldview of the Novel," an essay by Broch from which Pérez Gay translates the following passage:

> If there exist moral exigencies in art—and a brief stroll through artistic circles should be enough to convince anyone that they are indeed necessary—they should be formulated in the manner of prohibitions: "One should not imitate in part or whole other

> works of art, for in this case one will create kitsch"; or "One should not work with an inordinate concern for the results, for in this case one will create kitsch"; and finally, "One should not confuse the work of art with adherence to dogmatic principles for the production of said work, for in this case one will certainly produce kitsch." One who produces kitsch is not one whose production is an inferior kind of art, nor one who is partially or totally ignorant of art, for such a person cannot be measured according to the standards of aesthetics, rather we must accept—now, as you may have guessed, we find ourselves in the realm of talking films and operetta—that we are definitely dealing with a morally degraded person, a delinquent with evil inclinations and no scruples. Or, to put it in less pathetic terms, such a person is decidedly a pig. And we draw this conclusion based on the fact that kitsch represents evil within the realm of art. Would you prefer an archetypal example of kitsch? Nero playing his lute before the bodies of Christians enveloped in flames: He is the archetypal dilettante, an authentic esthete who sacrifices everything in his intent to create an aesthetic effect. The true artist, on the contrary, is not concerned with sublime effects. His only concern is diligence.

This must be one of the most lamentably sincere passages Broch wrote. In the first place, the image of Nero he evokes seems to me not "archetypal" kitsch but kitsch internalized in the POV of the author: everything is sacrificed for the sake of rhetorical effect; it is almost as perfect in its parodic reach as the Jewish fantasy in the scene from *Inglourious Basterds* where Adolf Hitler dies during a massacre of Nazi leaders. But, still more importantly, the entire passage has a strong whiff of embittered authoritarian nihilism. The petitio principii related to art borders on the impossible: not even Joyce, Pound, or Eliot would have been capable of approving of it, let alone Kurosawa, Fritz Lang, or John Ford. In essence, what Hermann Broch calls kitsch art is what we would call tradition.

This problem (of tradition and the sublime or, as Eliot terms it, of "tradition and the individual talent") will become a constant preoccupation throughout the twentieth century. Harold Bloom was the cultural figure charged with formulating a systematic response to it, and he did this by generating a complete theory of literature in which the relationships of power between works and authors do not correspond solely to the avatar of the sublime (the canonical), but also to that of parody; in Bloom's coinage, "the anxiety of influence." For Bloom, the history of literature revolves around an age-old contest in which writers quote one another, re-create and challenge one another; self-parody; invent precursors; steal and plagiarize subjects, techniques, and visions; so constructing a corpus of superior works, and also a relational frame for reading, psychoanalysis, and interpretation. T. S. Eliot parodies Shakespeare in a negative sense in the first verse of "A Game of Chess," the second canto of *The Waste Land*, but he also parodies Dante (in a positive sense) throughout his *Four Quartets*.

Many critics believe that Bloom's work is nothing more than an attempt to oust Eliot from his throne as the dominant English-language literary censor of his day. The main objective of this—apparently successful—exercise in usurpation was not so much to erase the figure of Eliot as to emend the political construction of the Western canon: if Dante was the greatest Western poet for Eliot, for Bloom it was Shakespeare. This political campaign fought over parody and the sublime is the common driving force behind three major books written by Bloom: *The Anxiety of Influence*, *The Western Canon*, and *Shakespeare*.

Enough of gringo professors and Austrian industrialist-novelists. What I'm trying to say is that Q's narrative technique—the sum of references, quotations, and plagiarism—is nothing new; it is located at the center of the artistic tradition to which we belong and, moreover, has stylistic features also to be found in the works of Eliot, Joyce, and Mikhail Bulgakov, to mention just three writers without whom it would be impossible to understand twentieth-century art. The difference is that Q distills his influences from B movies, the subgenres of exploitation film, memorabilia, gore, cartoons: kitsch art in high doses, world fragments that were not sublime until they came into his hands. This simple demiurgic skill alone would be enough to place Tarantino among the great contemporary masters of the tension between parody and the sublime. But Q also added a Shakespearean element to the formula: the revelatory soliloquy, that obsolete dramatic technique that Bloom, in his genius, describes as "self-overhearing": the character overhears himself.

—

I dreamed that my job consisted of transcribing complaints by fictional characters about their creators. I still had my old typewriter. I'd been assigned a station at the end of a red corridor. My clientele stood in a long line before me. Some were white dragons with long mustaches like octopus tentacles, others resembled moldy statues of presidential dwarves with permanent smiles carved in stone, yet others were wearing Oscar de la Renta suits. I filled in a form for each of them, adding the specific complaint in the box at the bottom of the page—the majority were related to physical attributes; very few of these beings mentioned their woes or adventures—stamped the document, gave the complainant a copy, and placed the original on a metal tray. A boring bureaucratic job that not even the outlandish appearances of most of my service users could enliven.

An explosion woke me up. It seemed to be at some distance, perhaps near the entrance to the underground complex. Something in my body recognized the frequency of the sound: "A bazooka," I said. I stood up and made straight for my walk-in closet, where I took off my pajamas and put on a Nike tracksuit: I had no desire to repeat the experience of finding myself in the street inappropriately dressed. A few moments later, one of Jacobo Montaña's attendants came into my bedroom. He had a 12-guage Remington Wingmaster shotgun slung over his shoulder and was carrying a bulletproof vest.

"We need to get the fuck out of here, sir. They're blitzing us."

Without waiting for a reply, he strapped the vest around my torso and pushed me toward the exit. We crossed the plastic garden, where some of Montaña's men were repelling what I recognized, even at that distance, as a squadron of the Mexican Naval Infantry, and headed down the main corridor, away from the entrance to the bunker.

"Where are we going?"

"There's another exit that comes out on gringo soil. Just follow me and don't ask questions."

Those were my guide's last words: a bullet entered the back of his neck and took his left eye out.

I decided to crawl on my belly along the floor, as I'd seen in thousands of action movies. Lead, dust, and pieces of concrete were flying around me. I had no idea which way to go. I followed the long corridor, turned into the storage area, and reached the room that housed the basketball court. There, I got to my feet and opened the door. Inside, sitting in the bleachers, was Jacobo Montaña. He was wearing his everlasting Rosa Gloria Chagoyán terry cloth bathrobe and hugging a bulletproof vest as if it was a teddy bear.

"The pigs have tracked you down, champ. Congratulations."

The words were spoken with bitterness, but also with a weariness that indicated a vein of sick joy.

The feds and the marines burst into the room in military formation. I knelt in the middle of the court and clasped my hands behind my neck, as I'd also seen in thousands of movies.

It's midday on the streets of Los Angeles. An olive-green two-door Maverick '74 is traveling west along Beverly Boulevard, approaching North La Brea. Gildardo is at the wheel. Rosendo is in the front passenger seat.

"Who told you?" asks Gildardo.

"I found it on the internet."

"Since when did you start using the net? Weren't you fired from telecommunications command?"

"I found it, right?"

Gildardo twists his mouth in a gesture of scorn.

"Seeing is believing."

"He's the fucking owner of the movie theater, OK? He'll have to turn up there sooner or later. And if he doesn't, we take one of the employees and plank him till he gives us the home address."

The Maverick passes the New Beverly Cinema and stops, engine still running, a few yards from the property. Over the entrance, a banner with bright red lettering on a luminous white background reads: "HAPPY BIRTHDAY QUENTIN KILL BILL THE WHOLE BLOODY AFFAIR."

"I can't park here."

"Don't. Keep the engine running and the blinkers flashing. I'll go investigate. A couple of minutes, no longer."

Rosendo opens the door on the passenger side and starts to get out, but Gildardo grabs the lapel of his jacket to detain him.

"Just tell me one thing. Why are we doing this?"

"Doing what?"

Rosendo seems confused.

"This."

"The job?"

"The job."

"A job's a job, that's what you said. Someone's gotta do it."

"Yeah. But look at us: we cross the border, drive to L.A. to take out some famous dude just 'cause Jacobo Montaña's got a piece of dry snot worrying his brain."

"If Montaña says he wants the head of Quentin Tarantino, we take him the head of Quentin Tarantino. Don't think about it, don't try to change the date of the test, don't piss around wasting time the way you were doing with Melanie: you just do the job you've been given. And that's it. The day we start questioning orders, we'll be living like animals and end up killing each other."

Rosendo makes another attempt to get out of the Maverick and Gildardo stops him once more.

"Montaña's been taken."

Silence.

"When?"

"It was on Telemundo a while ago. The pigs blew up the bunker. They're flying him to Organized Crime right now."

"Call Dante Mamulique."

"I already did. He said to go on as planned until further orders."

"So there you are. What part didn't you understand?"

"It's not like we're about to take out some journalist or a bolero singer, Rosendo. Have you seen this man's movies? He loves samurais. He must have a whole fucking army of them for protection."

Rosendo takes out his .357 Magnum and inspects the magazine, barrel, and trigger.

"I couldn't give a rat's ass about samurais. That's why I travel armed."

He returns his weapon to its holster.

The entrance to the New Beverly Cinema is deserted. From inside, a man with Latino features runs out. He's tattooed, is wearing a muscle shirt, and is carrying a semiautomatic firearm. A uniformed police officer appears behind him; he's pulling out a regulation pistol as he runs.

In the Maverick, Rosendo says:

"Here's how it's gonna be: we're gonna find Tarantino. We're gonna cut off his head, like we were ordered. And we're gonna take it back to Mexico and hand it in a gift box to Don Jacobo Montaña. Or to whatever motherfucker's in charge of the cartel when we get there. Period."

Rosendo gets out of the car. The tattooed Latino runs toward him, with the uniformed police officer in pursuit. Sirens sound in the distance. The tattooed Latino gives a half-turn and fires at the police officer. The officer fires back. Twice. A stray bullet hits Rosendo in the leg. Rosendo drops to the sidewalk, extracts his gun from his shoulder holster, and opens fire: his first bullet hits the tattooed Latino between the eyes, the second gets the police officer in the chest. The sirens are getting louder.

Gildardo jumps out of the Maverick and attempts to help Rosendo to stand. Patrol cars grind to a halt, surrounding them. The uniformed officers shield themselves behind the doors of their vehicles and take aim at the sicarios.

"Police," shouts a nasal voice above the confusion of sirens, moans, hammers being de-cocked, threats, and banging doors. "Drop your weapons."

Rosendo shoots at the officers. Gildardo takes his gun from its holster and follows his example. The officers return fire: bullets hail down on the two bodies until both Rosendo and Gildardo fall lifeless to the ground.

Members of the LAPD approach cautiously. The red lettering of the banner over the entrance to the New Beverly Cinema is unscathed. It reads: "HAPPY BIRTHDAY QUENTIN KILL BILL THE WHOLE BLOODY AFFAIR."

Harold Bloom says that William Shakespeare was the inventor of *the human*. Put that way, the idea sounds weird, but what Bloom is referring to—not without a degree of baroque adornment and exaggeration—is the modern emergence of a metahumanity: the invention of fictional characters with profound psyches, beings not only capable of self-awareness but also with access to sudden revelations of the unconscious. In broad outline, Bloom's theory is that pre-Shakespearean characters are not completely individuated but depend on such conventions as destiny, hubris (the vice of exaggerated pride that characterizes classical Greek heroes), symbolic representations, allegory (Dante), themes (for example, the king's favorite knight who falls in love with his new queen), and so on: they are, in the end, social conceptions poured into the molds of individual people. By contrast, Bloom insists, Shakespearean characters gradually detach themselves from the mold and the material that filled it to acquire a status that, in some pain-filled way, makes them similar to humans, no longer taken en bloc but one by one: they are characters with cognitive power. Pedro A. Jaramillo defines this power as “the mode in which each individual classifies knowledge to establish an internal mental order . . . : one of the keys to personality. It is the basis for any understanding of the reactions of individuals at a given moment, and the soundness of their judgments.” Shakespearean characters are, then, more *mimetic* than those of preceding eras; their capacity for imitating flesh-and-blood humans (their parody: their *parallel ode*) is complex and credible. The most noteworthy features of a written character with cognitive power are, on the one hand, doubt (since self-determination and free will are social phantoms, while doubt is inherent in absolutely anybody at all: Am I really awake? Did that really happen last night or are my senses deceiving me?). And on the other, desire and change: a mimetic character is not what he is but what he wants. And, because he wants a lot of things, he cannot always be the same; his essential nature is imprecise.

So far this is just stating the obvious, and that is why, historically, the best way to exemplify it has been through Hamlet’s soliloquy. A man argues with himself about the appropriateness of being or not being, about the dreamlike or real nature of death, and about whether the weight of the latter is due to panic in the face of nothingness or something more subtle: the possibility that there might be, beyond life, a more profound primordial horror than nothingness. Harold Bloom’s ideas don’t at this point appear entirely detached from the Western critical tradition. But he goes on to say that what adds a further dimension to Hamlet’s words is not his solemn demeanor: it is the fact that the character overhears himself as he speaks those words. That is to say, in any literary piece influenced by oratory, the characters know in advance what they are going to say. It is as if their consciousness had already, for a long time, been writing, rewriting, and rehearsing the lamentations and prayers they direct to the gods. In Shakespeare, by contrast—I’m still channeling Bloom here—when the character says something and we, the audience, hear it for the first time, the character is also hearing himself say that thing for the first time. And, on saying it, he discovers it: discovers a central aspect of his personality. At this point, the writing is no longer oratory but psychoanalysis. That is why Bloom considers Shakespearean creations to be the grand antecedent to the work of Freud. And that is also the reason for not only their strangeness but also their familiarity.

I don't intend to linger on a clarification of how far my theories about Shakespeare coincide with Bloom's; I will say only that "self-overhearing" is a rhetorical figure that appears in certain passages of the book of Job. What I would like to point out—to put the finishing touches on this brief summary of my master's thesis—is that one of the principle ingredients of Q's work is parody of the Shakespearean soliloquy constructed from pop references. I could give various examples (Jules in the coffee shop attempting, with rabbinic eagerness, to elucidate a misquoted passage from the Bible stands out for me), but I believe the most perfect of all is Bill's soliloquy. Speaking to Beatrix Kiddo, his loved one and enemy, the character says:

> As you know, I'm quite keen on comic books. Especially the ones about superheroes. I find the whole mythology surrounding superheroes fascinating. Take my favorite superhero, Superman. Not a great comic book, not particularly well drawn. But the mythology . . . The mythology is not only great; it's unique. . . . Now, a staple of the superhero mythology is, there's the superhero and there's the alter ego. Batman is actually Bruce Wayne, Spider-Man is actually Peter Parker. When that character wakes up in the morning, he's Peter Parker. He has to put on a costume to become Spider-Man. And it is in that characteristic Superman stands alone. Superman didn't become Superman. Superman was born Superman. When Superman wakes up in the morning, he's Superman. His alter ego is Clark Kent. His outfit with the big red "S," that's the blanket he was wrapped in as a baby when the Kents found him. Those are his clothes. What Kent

> wears—the glasses, the business suit—that's the costume. That's the costume Superman wears to blend in with us. Clark Kent is how Superman views us. And what are the characteristics of Clark Kent. He's weak . . . he's unsure of himself . . . he's a coward. Clark Kent is Superman's critique on the whole human race. Sorta like Beatrix Kiddo and Mrs. Tommy Plympton. . . . You would've worn the costume of Arlene Plympton. But you were born Beatrix Kiddo. And every morning when you woke up, you'd still be Beatrix Kiddo.

"Are you calling me a superhero?" she asks, and Bill replies, "I'm calling you a killer."

What is the character actually talking about? Of course, when he describes his former girlfriend, Bill is describing himself, as in one of those spectacular multiple-dream images where, according to Lacan, all characters are the Ego. That already entails a literary refinement that transcends the stylized hyperviolence of the film. Nevertheless, the soliloquy reaches its apogee in the analysis of comic books: when Bill describes Superman, he is, between the lines, describing the Nietzschean superman, the one who rises above "herd morality" and the death of God to construct a new world. A world that, in one of its most poorly planned dystopias, ended in Nazism. The analogy between the killer and the superman isn't new (there's at least one other memorable movie that addresses it: Hitchcock's *Rope*). But the Shakespearean mechanism Q employs to address it (the character overhears himself) makes it sadder and darker; makes it sublime.

I was allowed to visit him three months and seventeen days after my rescue from the bunker. The man at Organized Crime initially said that his no was final, but I bribed him with the promise to write and publish a report of my rescue, brimful of praise for the forces of law and order, exaggerating their courage, and describing their war on the narco trade as "the political project of one of the most brilliant, most courageous statesmen in the history of Mexico." A pack of lies in exchange for Jacobo Montaña's curriculum vitae, I can now say.

I had to take a long flight and then travel overland to a maximum-security rehabilitation center, the location of which I am not at liberty to reveal. As this was just two weeks before the much-publicized extradition to the United States of the most powerful Mexican drug baron, everyone around us was on edge. I was frisked at the entrance to the facility as though I was the prisoner. They allowed me to take in a pencil, a notebook, and a small digital recorder. I was escorted along concrete corridors—a brief, fond déjà vu of our bunker—to a room that was empty except for a pair of chairs fixed to the floor and separated by a large sheet of safety glass. I sat down on my side of the court and waited for a quarter of an hour until Jacobo was brought in. He was cuffed at the wrists and ankles and wearing a gray uniform, somewhere between pajamas and mechanics' overalls. They led him to the seat on the other side of the glass, attached his cuffs to rings embedded in the floor and wall, and left us "alone": by which I mean alone aside from the array of audiovisual security equipment.

We sat looking at each other in silence for several minutes, not knowing how to start.

"Rosendo and Gildardo are dead," I said to break the ice.

"I heard," replied Montaña, unmoved.

Closely shaved, his straight hair cut short and peppered with gray at the temples and brow, bespectacled, he looked like a portrait of an aged Richie Gecko.

Silence fell between us again. Out of sheer nerves I began to doodle in my notebook. Time was running out. Defeated, I said:

"You have to tell me."

"Tell you what?"

I was aware that he was playing innocent just to watch me seethe. But I also noticed in his voice an anxiousness to talk to someone he knew, someone familiar and unworthy of respect, someone from the time when he was an all-powerful ruler. I tried again.

"You have to tell me why you put a price on Quentin Tarantino's head."

Jacobo emitted a deeply unconvincing laugh.

Then, against all the odds, he started to unleash the soliloquy I'd been aching to hear for months.

"The story I'm going to tell you happened a long time ago. It's about a robbery at a warehouse, about an armed assault planned by an officer of the judicial police to take revenge on his lover, about a woman dressed as Muñequita Elizabeth handcuffed to a bed in the Hotel de los Beisbolistas, about a code of honor based on abuse, and a walk among the dead any Sunday night. But it's also about how a person who one day went to the movies with his ex-girlfriend ended up being me. I'm going to tell you that story because I love you but don't know you. There's just one condition: turn off the tape recorder. You'll have to reconstruct it from memory.

"First you need to know a few things. I was never some hick *gomero*; I'm not one of those kids born in the hills who start growing poppies just to survive and end up as narcos because they've got no other choice. No way. I was born into a middle-class urban family and when I finished high school I went to the capital to study acting. I was twenty-four and a NEET the first time I fired a pistol.

"That night, I went to see a movie with Bertha. Don't ask me what was showing; some kind of horror film. I'd just returned to Saltillo after an absence of four years and, up until then, had seen hardly any of my old acquaintances. At first, while we were crossing the carpeted lobby, blowing my few remaining pesos on candy and the last available seats in the central section, I tried to behave like a well-brought-up, educated young man; she was my friend, no longer my girlfriend. But she had that smell of violet-flavored gum and clean sweat that, according to Olague, my character-development teacher, you can almost taste in your mouth when you know a *sensual moment* is coming. I spent half the evening trying to get my hand under her blouse. Bertha resisted with a strength that made me even hornier; she stamped on my foot and complained about the taste of my spit.

"We left the theater a little after ten. Sunday: deserted streets, a car radio emitting *La Hora Nacional* and, farther off, another playing Soda Stereo rock; it was the spring of ninety-one, champ. I invited Bertha to my place, but the bitch said she'd prefer to make her own way home. I found her a cab.

"I walked west through Victoria to get some air and visit the neighborhood where I used to hang out with my high school crowd. Before I reached Xicoténcatl, a voice called the name I had at that time. I soon discovered that it was Benja's voice. By his side, in the shadows of the García department store, were Chota and Piel. I greeted them warmly but Benja gestured at me to be quiet.

"'We'll celebrate when it's over, bro.'

"'What's over?'

"'I'll explain in a moment. You're a godsend.'

"A patrol car pulled up to the sidewalk. Chota moved to the window and spoke to the driver for a few seconds. The car moved away.

"'They're up for it,' said Chota, 'but they want five pieces each.'

"'OK,' Benjamín replied.

"The tension among my old gang eased. Something told me I should make myself scarce, but then someone else put an arm around my shoulder.

"'So what's up, movie star? We thought you were in Hollywood, you bastard.'

"That was Piel. He spun me around. When I hugged him back, he gasped in pain and pushed me away.

"'Take it easy. Can't you see I'm wounded?' He lifted his T-shirt to show me six stiches in his torso. 'I got into a fight with Piedra and he put the knife in.'

"Benjamín asked where I'd been. 'To a movie,' I said.

"'Sexy chick?'

"'The chick's Bertha.'

"'The baker?'

"We'd called her that since we were kids. Her family owned El Pez que Fuma, the local bakery, but for us that nickname had nothing to do with her dad's profession; it referred to her white thighs, her short stature, the breasts that were too large for her slim frame. She was fourteen when, after a great deal of pleading on my part, she agreed to date me. We were together for two months and then she told me to go to hell: she assured me that I couldn't love her anymore because she'd two-timed me and lost her virginity. 'It's no big deal,' I said, mustering the courage of a teenager who thinks he's capable of killing. *I forgive you.* But she liked the other guy better.

"'The very same,' I replied.

"No one said anything, but we all knew that Benjamín had been the first person to fuck Bertha.

"'Like I said, you're a godsend, with that dumbass getting himself cut,' said Benja, pointing to Piel. 'Are you in?'

"'Put me in the picture first.'

"'Right across the street there's a warehouse. Stereos, TV sets, cassette recorders: all Japanese. The goods are hot, no one's going to make a report. We have to get in and out through the roof.'

"'And transport?'

"'You just saw it: the patrol car.'

"'It won't be big enough. And how are we going to get the stuff down?'

"'We've brought a small cage and rope. But with any luck we won't need them.'

"It was a lousy plan, champ, whichever way you looked at it. But I'd just bounced back in from Mexico City without a centavo to my name, drama school finished and no job.

"'Do I have to go up? Isn't there anyone else?'

"'No. Piel can't do it; he's the lookout.'

"'OK, just for a laugh,' I lied.

"'That and more,' said Chota.

"At around eleven Piel went to the corner to keep watch on both streets, and the rest of us climbed the two stories of the building to the night watchman's room on the roof. Through a sliding window—lined with sheets of cardboard in place of glass—filtered the chords of a bolero. I peered through a gap in the cardboard: an old man wearing a filthy *guaripa* was lying on a folding bed watching a portable TV. He'd pulled down his pants and shorts so he could scratch his balls.

"The door burst open. Chota entered the room, got the old man in a neck hold, and held an ice pick in front of his eyes.

"'Don't make a move, you bastard. Don't turn around.'

"'What you whisperin' for? You made enough noise kickin' in the door?'

"'Shut your mouth.'

"'This is Don Hildebrando's warehouse, son.'

"'Keep it fucking shut.' He moved the ice pick closer to the man's eyes.

"'Yeah, sure thing, but don't be mean: gimme a chance to pull up my shorts.'

"Chota let him go.

"'Just keep your cool, pop,' said Benja from outside. 'Give the keys to my friend there and you won't even know we were here.'

"'It's Don Hildebrand's place,' repeated the man. 'We got wind you were coming. You're the guys who been hangin' around across the street, right?'

"Chota pricked his cheek with the ice pick. The old guy fumbled in his pocket.

"'Here's the damn keys. But they're only for the second floor, and those whatever-you-call-'ems are too big for the stairway.'

"While Chota was keeping watch on the old man, Benjamín and I opened the hatch and went down into the building. The watchman had been telling the truth: our only access was a spiral staircase. The main way out of the warehouse was one floor below and consisted of a long corridor leading to a metal curtain. Even if we'd had the keys, the noise of opening it would have attracted attention.

"I asked Benja if he'd brought a flashlight. He said he hadn't. We had to do the whole thing in the dark, flicking our lighters now and again.

"We tried carrying a single gadget between the two of us. All the TV sets and larger stereos were too big for the spiral staircase, so we had to make do with the small or medium-sized stuff. Keeping your footing in the dark was no easy matter. As we ascended the stairs, the edges of the metal steps tore at the packing cases, making a fucking mess of them. We found a few high-tech cassette recorders, and Benja came across a collection of six car stereo systems. We put them in a black garbage bag.

"After moving the goods up to the roof, we had to find a way to get them down to the street. That was real tough because we had rope and a sort of cage, but no tackle block or gloves, and even though the goods weren't very heavy, Benja and I ended up with our hands covered in rope burns. On one of the trips, the cage tipped over and a TV set fell to the ground, almost landing on Piel's head. We finally managed to get out three TVs, four cassette recorders, two home stereo systems, and the six car stereos Benja had scavenged.

"The whole job took over an hour, and then we stopped to catch our breath. I flattened myself against a parapet between two buildings and Benja lay down on the square cover of a water tank. The boleros on the watchman's TV continued to float through the air. In the moonlight, the outlines of the buildings made stepped patterns in space, and piles of broken glass sparkled on nearby rooftops; I remember that because I thought it was somehow like seeing the sound of crickets. If, at that moment, I'd had a few beers on hand, I wouldn't have minded spending the rest of the night up there. It was like returning to times when Granma and Gramps used to take me to La Boca dam on vacation, and at night—while they were talking about ghosts and swatting the mosquitoes biting at their feet in the dark—I'd amuse myself watching the lemon-yellow flickering of fireflies on the water.

"That feeling was short-lived. The patrol car arrived. We went to find Chota, freed the watchman, descended by the air-con system, and slid down the gutter to the sidewalk.

"'What the hell are you guys playing at?' said one of the officers.

'We've already driven around the block three times. The feds could turn up any second now and you're fooling around up there.'

"'Fuck this,' said the other cop, who was checking the goods. 'Japanese, you said Japanese. These are just Chinese rip-offs.'

"'Hey, no problem,' said Benja. 'We'll sort things out later.'

"The second officer found the bag with the car stereos, hauled it out, and got into his vehicle.

"'These are ours. We're out of here. God alone knows the mess that crap's gonna get you into.'

"'Is there any water around here?' I asked Piel. 'I want to wash up.'

"'There's a wall hydrant a bit farther along. I'll come with you.'

"'Make it quick,' ordered Benja. 'Super quick.' Then, turning to the cop, he said, 'Don't be assholes. Give us a ride to Topo Chico, we'll divvy it up and go our own ways.'

"'You kidding?' said the second cop. 'You're in the shit. Partner, tell 'em to go to hell.'

"Piel opened the faucet and washed his hands and face. I did the same. I had my eyes shut under the stream of water when I heard the screech of tires. I raised my head and saw a white Chevy parked near the other members of our group. Two dark figures emerged. Another car pulled up beside me. Piel made to run, but a third figure leaped from the car, tackled him, lifted him by the collar, and punched him twice.

"'Please, take it easy. I've got a knife wound.' Piel attempted to raise his T-shirt to show his stitches but the other man must have thought he was trying to reach for a weapon, because he twisted his arm, pushed him against the wall, and continued punching him until, in the streetlight, he saw that his knuckles were stained red. Then he stopped. Piel's body slumped onto the asphalt. Another two figures got out of the car.

"I turned to face the wall with my hands behind my head and legs apart, as I'd seen in the movies. The water was still running from the faucet. My pants were wet. Behind me, a voice said:

"'Hey, Chacón. This one's not so dumb. I want him in the Cutlass with me when we get to the crime scene.'

"'Yes, sir.'

"My first thought was that the voice sounded scarily calm. My second was that it was going to be embarrassing to appear before the prosecutor with my pants and shoes soaked, as if I'd wet myself from fright when they arrested me.

"Benja and Chota had already been overpowered by the squad from the Chevy. There were six judicials in all. They herded us into a group, frisked us, and slapped us around a bit. Then they loaded us into the pickup and handcuffed us to a horizontal steel bar soldered to the cab. One of the cops tried to save the situation.

"'Hey, listen, this is our arrest. It's petty theft.'

"'I'm Captain Aldana.'

"'Sir. At your service, captain.'

"'I've got business with this bunch,' said Aldana. 'They're wanted for armed robbery of federal gas stations. Best thing you can do is get back on patrol and forget you ever saw them. I don't want Don Hildebrando getting the wrong idea when he sees this mess . . . Clear up the frigging crap, will you?' And he kicked one of the television sets we'd stolen.

"The uniformed officers did as they were told.

"'Noriega, drive these gentlemen to the planned location. Take Chacón and Muerto with you.'

"That was when our real Sunday started.

"The second time Bertha and I dated, it lasted a weekend. I was in senior high at the Narváez and her parents had enrolled her in a private Catholic school, so we'd seen very little of each other over the years. But one day our two schools joined up for a trip to the San Lorenzo Canyon, organized by an environmental agency to encourage ecological awareness among young people. It was a disaster: we ended up starting a fire.

"I'd been thinking of showing her that she wasn't the only fish in the sea, but right from the start she followed me everywhere, and don't get the idea that she wasted time trying to explain things: the night of our arrival she came to the tent I was sharing with a classmate. Wearing almost nothing. She didn't give a shit if we were seen or heard. That Friday was the first time we had sex. Then, early Saturday morning, she volunteered us to gather firewood and fetch water. We fucked in the nude on a boulder about a hundred and twenty feet above the camp. While she was going at it on my thighs, making incoherent sounds, her head thrown back to the sky, I was staring down into the void to frighten myself into not coming too soon. Later, while she was jumping on a thick branch to detach it from its trunk and so speed up the firewood gathering, Bertha said:

"'Doesn't this tree we're trying to kill look beautiful?'

"First thing on Sunday morning, the forest rangers kicked us out of the canyon. The school buses took us as far as Alameda Zaragoza, where our families were waiting for us. In the seat beside me, Bertha pointed out of the window and said:

"'Hey, there's my boyfriend,' and she waved to the crowd of people huddled together by the Lago de la República.

"She gave me a quick kiss and said goodbye. Then she got off the bus and flung herself on some guy. It could have been any guy: I can't even remember his face. She kissed him—that I do remember—as if she'd spent the whole trip missing him . . .

"And that's what I was recalling as the judicials were driving us across the city in a pickup. We were heading for a stretch of waste-land in the Ramos Arizpe industrial estate. We didn't say a word the whole journey; Benja and Chota looked panicked and Piel was out for the count.

"When we reached our destination, they lined us up beside the pickup. Two other vehicles were parked nearby. They put on *grupera* music, opened cans of beer and a bottle of Buchanan's. Every now and then they threatened us with pistols, joking about letting us run and then shooting us while we were making our escape. Piel was still lying in the pickup, shaking with fever.

"After about an hour, Aldana and his driver turned up in a Cutlass. The captain got out and looked us over.

"'Do you know what's back there?' he asked, nodding to the hills.

"After a moment's silence Chota replied:

"'No, we don't, sir.'

"'This one's got manners,' said Captain Aldana in a pleased tone. 'Speak when you're spoken to. What we've got back there is our burial ground. How many graves so far, Chueca?'

"Chueca, the captain's driver, replied:

"'Around forty-three, sir.'

"'Forty-three,' repeated Aldana. 'So we don't forget.'

"'So we don't forget, sir,' parroted Chueca.

"'Now you know: so no tricks. Noriega, explain it to them.'

"Noriega took a step forward and instructed us with the seriousness of someone addressing a deployment about to undertake an important mission.

"'It's very simple: you're under arrest for the armed robbery of federal gas stations. Only you haven't committed the infringement yet; we're going to give you the equipment you need and take you to the scene of the crime. You do your stuff, we arrest you, and that's it. Tomorrow you'll be sleeping peacefully in lockup.'

"It sounded even crazier to us than it must to you, champ. But that was Aldana's plan.

"While we were getting ready to board the vehicles, Muerto explained to his boss that Piel was badly hurt. They decided it was too risky to use him and, anyway, three would be enough for the heist.

"'Keep him with you, Muerto,' ordered the captain. 'We'll see how we can involve him later.'

"They worked out the logistics: I'd travel in the car with Aldana, with Chueca driving; Benja and Chota would go in a Shadow, guarded by Chacón and someone called Jonás; Muerto would be in the Chevy with Piel to make it seem like the whole squad had arrived in that vehicle; and Noriega would be on sentry duty a couple of miles from the gas station, with his radio on in case of unexpected eventualities.

"'Did you bring supplies, boss?'

"Aldana put an ounce of cocaine on the hood of the Chevy.

"'Offer some to the kids too. You have to give them an incentive, the way you do with hookers.'

"As we were walking to the Cutlass and the Shadow we were going to use for the heist—both pretty beat-up—Aldana approached me and said:

"'I've seen you somewhere before, foxy eyes. You kind of remind me of the guy in the advertisement. Remember? The ostrich.'

"'Yeah, it's him,' said Chueca.

"'How can you tell?' I asked.

"'My cousin knows you. You were at the ICH with him. Then you went to Mexico City, right?'

"'Right.'

"'So that's how.'

"Champ, you've no idea how much I wanted to kill that agent of law and order for making me remember the glory and the farce. No idea just how much I wanted to return to the doors of the production company and shout that it was a mistake to let me go, beg some invisible person to take pity on me and not put me back on the streets among those schmucks. Yes, television had made me popular, but I was also a laughingstock for those morons: a bunch of losers who would end up devouring me with zombie jealousy.

"When I was twenty-two, I made a commercial. My thirty seconds of fame.

A handheld camera. In the foreground, a fifties ranch and a presenter. Behind, a corral filled with ostriches.

'Here we are with Don Fernando de Ceballos, pioneer and spokesperson for ostrich farming in America.'

A hand (apparently the cameraman's) enters the frame.

'What's that?' asks an off-mike voice.

The camera tracks unsteadily toward the part of the corral where I, surrounded by ostriches, have my head in a hole.

'What's the problem, youngster?'

I cry. Gradually I reveal my face. Confusion: everyone—ostriches included—flees. Except for the camera, which continues recording my face at ground level: blotches, zits, warts, and hairs . . . I'm the classic monster from a Santo horror movie.

Voice-over:

'There's no need to hide: let us fix your problems. At Clínicas Larios we have the perfect solutions for all your skin problems.'

Cut.

I'm looking straight into the camera again, radiant, without a single blemish, surrounded by slender girls in miniskirts.

Close-up of my head and this triumphant phrase:

'Thanks to Larios, I can show my face: I'm not an ostrich anymore.'

"'Why did you come back?'" asked Chueca.

"I told the truth:

"'I graduated from drama school and couldn't get work as an actor.'

"'Why d'ya turn back, child, if you'd already won?' said Aldana imitating the voice of Piporro. 'Move your ass, man.'

"We got into the vehicles and set out in a convoy for the Monterrey highway. The captain was beside me in the back of the Cutlass.

"'I'm gonna let you in on what this is all about: it's revenge.'

"He said he was in love.

"'A really beautiful guy. You're quite good-looking, don't get me wrong, but he's . . . you can't imagine. And what a talent in bed. We were happy till he went and dropped me for the old lady of a state government minister. I can't compete with that during daylight hours. But I can make them pay.'

"I was as confused as you, champ. The thought of a killer like Aldana being in love with another man felt repugnant, and not because I care what people do with their asses, but in those days I was dumb enough to believe that brutes like him shouldn't fall in love with anyone. That's what you cultured people call irony, right?

"'I want you to know that you've got a special role in this whole business,' Aldana suddenly blurted out.

"I thought he was just trying to jerk me off, although for an instant I also harbored the hope that if I played along and managed to seduce him, I might save myself from jail.

"This is how it was going to work: Muerto would stop the Chevy just before the gas station. The occupants of the Shadow would park in front of the minimart, and the Cutlass would be a few yards away, right by the gas pumps. Chota and Benja would be inside the minimart carrying the weapons Jonás and Chacón would give them. Two minutes later, I'd go up to the only attendant in the station (it was just before two in the morning on Monday: there never used to be anyone on the road at that hour) and show him my gun, also provided by the feds. Then it would be a matter of waiting for our captors and following the instructions for our arrest.

"My friends went into the store and Chueca handed me a snub-nosed revolver. For an instant I fantasized about shooting him and Aldana, starting up the Cutlass, and getting out of there. But I'd never used a firearm. Aldana must have guessed what I was thinking, because he explained:

"'It isn't loaded.'

"I got out of the car holding the gun. It was windy: dust and willow leaves (I don't know why there were so many willow trees near the gas station) were gusting over the cracked asphalt. It wasn't cold; the air was unexpectedly mild. The area was well lit and looked safe, but the highway was deserted. Suddenly an off-track trailer passed; it was clattering and throwing off a stink of diesel that for some reason seemed to me an icy substance.

"I walked the length of the forecourt, as far as the last pump. Behind it, sitting on the concrete base with his arms crossed, a kid crammed into a PEMEX overall was dozing. I shuddered: he was well built, pure gym-trained muscle, and I thought that if I got too close, he might disarm me, beat me up, or put a bullet in me . . . I remembered that my weapon wasn't loaded. That gave me courage. I pointed the gun at him.

"'Freeze,' I said stupidly.

"The kid gave a start, got to his feet, and stood looking at me. He was tall. Young. Blond. As Aldana approached him from behind, I even managed to think that he did indeed have a handsome face.

"Aldana didn't kill him straight off. First he punched him in the ribs and then, when the kid doubled over in pain, he kicked his weight-bearing leg. The kid fell to the ground, faceup. Aldana took out his weapon, identical to mine, and fired at his balls.

"'Don't do it, darling,' sobbed the kid, covering his wound with both hands.

"'Fuck you, darling,' said Aldana and fired two shots into his chest.

"'Federal agents,'" said Chueca, standing behind me. 'On the ground.'

"'Freeze?' mocked Aldana. 'What kind of shit is that?'

"From the concrete, as Chueca was handcuffing me and attempting to get Muerto on the radio, I saw Benja and Chota coming out of the minimart with their wrists handcuffed behind their backs, escorted by agents Chacón and Jonás.

"Aldana grabbed my hair and lifted my head.

"'See how quick and easy that was, honey? You're charged with homicide now. Like I said, you've got a special role in this whole business.'

"They loaded us into our respective vehicles, we picked up Noriega—the lookout—by the side of the road, and the convoy set out for Saltillo. I thought they'd take us directly to the state prosecutor's office, but no: the bastards were in the mood to celebrate, so we went to the Hotel de los Beisbolistas.

"We drove through narrow, winding alleys in the center of the city: the old Tlaxcalteca neighborhood, made up of steep slopes and dilapidated adobe houses. We parked on a backstreet I'd never passed through (in those days, the city was so small and so old that whole stretches of it could get lost) and someone got out of his vehicle and opened the metal gates to a long carport. We parallel-parked. In the headlights of the Cutlass I made out a large patio at the far end, dominated by an acacia tree.

"They removed our cuffs and, slapping and punching us more out of habit than anything else, ordered us to get out of the cars. Muerto threw Piel—he was still semiconscious—over his shoulder.

"'Fuck this, guys,' said Chota. 'It's a frigging clandestine jail.'

"'Forward march, buddy,' said one of the judicials, giving him a whack. 'You can make your allegations later.'

"Two other agents, Chacón and Noriega, took their pistols from their holsters and silently escorted us to a side door. We passed through and, as the man in front of us switched on lights, saw one of those old houses with high ceilings, crumbling adobe walls mended with patches of cement, and a sort of corridor or covered patio with bedrooms on either side. It was a large tumbledown house with windows protected by ancient bars, just like the ones in Western jails. It had the general appearance of being some sort of hollow, oval thing but with corners . . . Like a huge adobe egg with prison windows, but a monstrous, rectangular egg made up of innumerable gray bedrooms with a long, narrow, peach-colored corridor in the center. The corridor was decorated with newspaper clippings, posters, and photos, either in wooden frames hanging from nails or thumbtacked to the walls. I scanned them as the officers led us to the bathroom (or maybe it was later, because, as you'll see, I made that journey a couple of times). There were portraits of Juan DeLiza, Nelson Barrera, Carlos Lee, El Gallo Batista, and Derek Bryant: baseball players who'd achieved short-lived fame in the early eighties. And big headlines: 'Ten innings and the crowd going wild,' 'Monclova has 5–3 record,' 'Another piece of devilry in the IMSS Park.'

"'Welcome to the Hotel de los Beisbolistas,' said Captain Aldana from the lounge. He flopped onto a couch and sprinkled a little coke onto a piece of glass. 'Make yourselves at home.'

"We were led farther down the corridor to a rectangular bathroom with glazed floral tiles, and equipped with a white toilet and bathtub veined with pale blue, old and elegant, despite the grime. The room was covered in cobwebs and dust, the floor carpeted in dirty paper, piss, and shit. There was a single barred window that looked out onto the acacia tree on the back patio. It was bathed in moonlight.

"They handcuffed Piel to the window bars, Benja to a pipe leading from the washbasin, and Chota to the remains of a wood-burning boiler in the corner. My cuffs were removed and I was ordered to sit on the toilet bowl. I was there for a good while, and this is what was going through my mind: in that corridor, on the way to the bathroom, I had the feeling I'd glimpsed someone through a half-open door, someone chained to a bed: she was wearing a doll's outfit, her face was made-up like a clown's, and she had a frizzy wig on her head. Or perhaps I didn't really see her at that moment; perhaps I saw only a shape on the mattress, and it was much later, when she put a pistol in my mouth, that I was able to examine her in detail. I'm not sure. Sometimes memory is like a video on rewind, a false premonition.

"Half an hour passed. From time to time music wafted into the bathroom, euphoric shouts and sobs. Chota, Benja, and I didn't exchange a single word: we were too tired, or terrified, or ashamed. Piel, on the other hand, began to regain consciousness. He sat up and asked:

"'Are we there?'

"Then he passed out again.

"Chueca appeared in the frame of the bathroom door and motioned for me to follow him. He led me to the room where we'd seen Captain Aldana. Behind me, I could hear the moans and cries of the woman dressed as Muñequita Elizabeth—this time I'm sure I did get a good look at her: she was being raped in full view by Chacón and Jonás. Aldana offered me a line of coke. I accepted. He offered me a glass of whisky. I accepted that too. He took me by the shoulders and pushed me to the door until I had a direct view of Muñequita's suffering.

"'We found her turning tricks on the corner of Valdés Sánchez and Abasolo,' he said. 'She might look like a clown, but she takes her clients to the Hotel Higaldo and robs them. You know how it is.'

"'No, I don't know.'

"'Maybe you do, maybe you don't,' he said without much interest. 'What matters is that you know what comes next, sweetheart.'

"We went back into the lounge and sat facing each other in armchairs.

"'Are they going to kill her?'

"Aldana's gesture seemed to say that anything was possible.

"'We're not sure yet. But we do know what's going to happen to you, right?'

"He took a revolver from his belt—I couldn't tell if it was his weapon or mine—and placed it on the table between us.

"'The story isn't over yet; not until the evidence comes before the public prosecutor's office. I'm wondering if you're willing to do something to make things a little easier for yourself.'

"'Whatever you say.'

"'See? That's what education does: you can adapt to any situation.'

"He got to his feet, unzipped his pants, told me to kneel, and forced me to give him a blow job. I tried not to think about what I was doing, watching out of the corner of my eye the torture of Muñequita in the room opposite. I guess her eyes met mine at some point, but my memory is hazy. Afterward, Captain Aldana told me to get up; he pulled down my pants and boxers, casually pushed me onto the sofa where he'd been sitting throughout, and began to fuck my ass. It was painful because we were both dry, but he didn't seem to care.

"I thought about the third time Bertha and I tried to get together. That was in eighty-nine. I'd been living in D.F. for two years and had just made my commercial for Clínicas Larios: the high point of my other life. It was Bertha's first time in the capital and I arranged to meet her in a really cool tamale restaurant in Condesa. Then we spent two days walking the city. I took her to see some of the ruined buildings still waiting to be demolished three years after the earthquake, and at night, we had dinner in some fairly cheap place before I took her to her hotel. We didn't fuck; just wound ourselves around each other at the door of her room. She said she needed to be sure, that she cared about me a lot, that she didn't want to have sex with me again unless it was for love and was the start of a lasting relationship . . . On the third day we went to a party given by some people from Coahuila living in D.F. Bertha got to talking to a young engineer from Sabinas and danced with him the whole night. They left together. Two months later they were married and the schmuck moved to Saltillo. The marriage lasted less than a year because he used to hit her. There were no children.

"I searched for any pretext not to think about my rape. For the second time, I noticed the revolver on the table. Was it mine or his? Was it loaded or empty? Captain Aldana was giving it to me harder and harder. I felt what I imagined to be blood (or it could have been sweat or shit or semen) trickling between my buttocks. When he was coming, I let myself fall onto my stomach and twisted around, my weight on one arm of the couch, and elbowed him in the nose. Before he could react, I chanced my hand: I grabbed the revolver from the table, took aim, and pulled the trigger. It was his. The bullet entered just below his nostrils, and his lower face opened up in a toothy rectangle like Schwarzenegger's predator. The people in the room next door—Jonás and Chacón raping Muñequita Elizabeth—were taken off guard: we glimpsed one another through the doors. First they went quiet. Then they leaped from the bed, looking for their weapons. What none of us knew at that moment—unfortunately for them—is that I'm a born deer hunter, champ. Never, since that first time, when I gave it to the captain, has my hand been unsteady. First I brought Jonás down with a bullet in the eye, then came Chacón, with two shots to his chest. Before exploring the rest of the Hotel de los Beisbolistas, I decided to put one last bullet into Captain Aldana, for good measure. I plugged him right in the center of his forehead. Not out of pity: it was for the disgust I felt at smelling my own shit on him.

"I put on my pants. Through the wall I could hear the other three agents—Chueca, Muerto, and Noriega—grabbing their weapons and loudly cursing each other and me. Chota and Benja were also screaming in the distance. Only Muñequita Elizabeth was silent; half-dressed, handcuffed to the bed, she was looking at me with those big makeup-smudged eyes. She and Piel.

"Someone was shooting an automatic; the bullets were soft-nosed and you could hear a dull thud as they hit the walls. I went out into the corridor: some of the pictures with baseball clippings had shattered and the glass cut into my belly as I crawled toward the bathroom. Noriega appeared out of one of the rooms farther along. He was holding a rifle. Without giving him time to take aim, I shot him in the cheek and, as he fell, put another slug right into his brain.

"I guessed I must be running short on ammo so I stuck the revolver in my belt and crawled toward the rifle. That's when Muerto hit me: the rebound from what I believe was a .38 glanced my ribs. Then he turned me over to see my face and put his Magnum to my head.

"'Motherfucking bastard motherfucker,' he screamed.

"Just when I was absolutely certain that Muerto was going to kill me, a bullet entered the back of his neck and exploded. His body fell beside mine. I struggled to sit up, only to find myself looking straight into the face of Muñequita Elizabeth. Or rather at her pistol: god knows how she'd managed to free herself from the cuffs and get hold of one of her rapists' weapons, but its barrel was now resting against my teeth. I didn't say a word, just raised my arms and let her cry.

"There was a sliding door behind her; through it I caught a glimpse of Chueca's back, his shoulders shaking as he attempted to open the door to the parking lot at the side of the building. Muñequita Elizabeth turned her head to face him. She moved the gun from my mouth and slid aside.

"I got to my feet and checked how many bullets I had left: the drum was empty. Muñequita Elizabeth—who was sitting on the floor, leaning back against the wall—held out her pistol. I took it.

"I had no idea how much ammo I had, champ, because in that other life I knew very little about semiautomatic weapons. All I did was check that the safety was off, the way I'd seen it done in movies. Instead of coming out with guns blazing—that day I learned that I don't like firing like a madman: I prefer taking out the enemy with minimum fuss—I waited. Crouching, I followed Chueca through the parking lot. I calculated that he'd try to start up the white Chevy, the last vehicle in the convoy, parked nearest the main gates.

I quickened my pace and, rather than confronting him head-on, slid beneath the chassis. From there, I heard the sound of a padlock and chain. Then the gates opening. I saw Chueca's feet getting into the Chevy and felt him settling himself behind the wheel. When I guessed he'd be ready to turn over the engine, I rolled to one side and stood by the window holding my weapon in both hands. God is good: he saw my face. I emptied the remaining ammo into him: four of five shots, I guess. Then I opened the driver's door and pulled the body out by one arm, just to give myself the pleasure of watching it fall into the dust.

"Muñequita Elizabeth passed beside me. She didn't turn her head to look but continued on through the gates and disappeared into the street. I never saw or heard of her again. I went back inside the Hotel de Beisbolistas to find my buddies.

"I searched Aldana's clothes for the key to the handcuffs and, in addition, found another bag of coke. In his shoulder holster I also discovered what is to this day my favorite firearm: a Glock 17. I did two lines, took the key and the holster, and went back down the corridor to the bathroom where my friends were chained. It was only then that I became aware of the sound of sirens and patrol cars in the distance.

"I managed to free Benja; he toppled into the bathtub, massaging his arms.

"'Thanks, bro,' he said, sobbing.

"Do you know what flashed into my mind at that moment, champ? *That sonofabitch fucked Bertha before I did.* I mean, I didn't even have to think about it.

"'This is for fucking Bertha before I did, you sonofabitch.'

"I killed him with two shots. Then I turned to Chota and, without even giving him time to react, I iced him, too, with a bullet to his brain. The one I did feel sorry about was Piel; he looked in a bad way. Still feverish, he sat up and again asked:

"'Are we there?'

"'We're there. Take it easy.'

"I put an arm under his shoulder and propped him against a piece of rotten wood lying beside the boiler, just to act as a cushion for the bullet. Then I aimed at the back of his head, and when I pulled the trigger, there was hardly a sound. In that short time I'd learned almost everything I needed to kill anyone at all.

"I stayed there a for moment looking sadly at the corpses of my friends. I still miss them.

"When I heard the patrol cars and shouts outside, I slipped the Glock 17 into its holster and escaped across the back patio. The sun was coming up. I passed the acacia I'd seen through the window. Its yellow flowers were so plump and neatly groomed. Have you ever seen them, champ? They smell beautiful in the spring. I jumped over a couple of walls and headed away from the Tlaxcalteca neighborhood to Topo Chico, where we'd all grown up together. To El Pez que Fuma.

"Did I make it to the bakery? 'Course I made it to the bakery, champ. Don't ask me why no one stopped an armed, bare-chested zombie, covered in blood, walking the streets of Saltillo at dawn. I guess it's one of those things that are getting more common in this country.

"It wasn't yet seven. Monday. The spring of ninety-one. As I'd supposed, Bertha and her mother were serving behind the counter while the old man was baking the second batch of *bolillos* in the backroom. Before going in, I took out the pistol. I wanted Bertha to get a good look at it. If she found out later what had happened, I wanted her to know who I was and what I was capable of, and I wanted her to live in fear of ever seeing me again. I went through the door. At first they just stared at me in surprise, but when they noticed the gun, they were alarmed. The old lady started to scream. Bertha motioned to her to be quiet and said:

"'What's up, darling? Are you OK?'

"I remembered Captain Aldana's last words to his boyfriend. *Fuck you, darling.* I picked up a *bolillo*. It was warm. I split it in two and took a bite. Then I remembered I had no money with me to pay so I put the Glock on the counter as a sort of offering or recompense for Bertha and her mother, and went off to finish my *bolillo*.

"That day I stopped being the ostrich from Clínicas Larios and I became Jacobo Montaña, the man who would later lead the bloodiest cartel in the country—according to the press. Executing Aldana was like eating his heart. What can I say? I became a hired killer; I informed, worked for the CIA, the DEA, trained with the Kaibiles in Guatemala, joined the army as part of a squadron formed to infiltrate the narco cartels; later, I allied myself to a drug baron; then I killed him and took over his business. A decade after that, I was caught and tried; thirty years they gave me, but I escaped from Loma Larga after two. Since then, I've lived underground. All this because of one Sunday night. I wasn't born a hick *gomero*: I wasn't some poor kid from the hills, champ; justice grew me up in a single working day.

"Things were going fine until your friend Tarantino turned up. The first time, I thought it was a joke or something worse: a trap. I'd rented an action movie and there I was on the screen; I go into a bar and start negotiating the sale of a few kilos of coke. My first thought was: That's not my voice. Then I begin to talk like crazy. I tell a bad joke and then someone puts a shot in the head of the guy sitting next to me; the blood splatters onto my face. I said to myself: That never happened. It took me about three movies to understand that I wasn't the ghost, that I had a double out there in the cinema world, and in this world too.

"I watched all the scenes, all the characters, and each one made me feel worse than before. I'd end up emptying my stomach into the toilet bowl, weak and shivering, but with a rage in my breast that on more than one occasion made me vent my fury on others. Once, I ordered around forty *pelados* to be killed in a *ranchito* (there was even a kid of fifteen), and I had their houses demolished with a backhoe and put their women on the street with nothing but what they were standing in. You know why? Because your friend Quentin appeared in a movie playing me as a crazy rapist murderer who ends up with vampires sucking his blood.

"They're nightmares; sketches in which you're either a devil or a moron, and then you end up dead. Because he always gets killed. It wears me out to think how many times I've died on-screen because of the asshole: Wasn't that enough to make me want to get my fucking own back? Don't you think a man needs his face to know who he is? Don't you think it's a personal affront for someone to go around with your face doing whatever the hell he wants?

"But that's not why I ordered the boys to bring me his head. That wasn't the reason. It was for something older and simpler: that scumbag stole my life. He's kind of like me in the movies, but in real life I wanted to be like him. I wanted to be an actor, to move from the Clínicas Larios commercial to TV and after that to cinema and, one day, to Hollywood. I'm like the mariachi in that other movie: I just wanted them to let me act. And you can bear having your appearance stolen, champ, but not the life you dream of. Am I right or what? I had to have him killed, had to have his head cut off for stealing the same thing Captain Aldana took from me that night in the Hotel de los Beisbolistas. And so I sent for you, and that's why the feds found me. Now I know what I should have done the very first time I saw him: torn off my own face. But what difference does it make now?"

Can pain educate without destroying? Are we made of the substance of fear? Could Jacobo Montaña overhear himself as he told me his story? Or is what Harold Bloom says about the character and his soliloquy a mere textual illusion? Sometimes I think the invention of the human is an egoistic blind spot we are incapable of making out; you can't be the fire and light it at the same time. Or can you? Those were the first questions that drummed in my mind as I was leaving the maximum-security prison where my kidnapper and host awaited extradition to the United States.

While Montaña was talking, I was able to see him again, not as the double of my favorite director, but in his real body: the body of a man around fifty who has dedicated half his life to torture. A murderer capable of taking out fifteen-year-olds in a fit of rage. A businessman who destroys homes with backhoes and poison. None of these activities made him less likable or interesting, and that's the worst of it: there's no more profound horror than an untroubled conscience.

I returned to Nuevo Laredo and my elderly aunt Rosa Gloria Chagoyán. Our house had been almost completely restored to its former state: my collections of classic DVDs and porn mags were gone forever, but the freshly painted concrete and partition walls were smooth and glossy, and the plumbing, light fixtures, and power sockets all functioned perfectly. It was as if the bazooka attack had never happened. In a weird form of courtesy, the Attorney General's office decided not to impound any of the things I'd acquired (or rather, that had been showered on me, paid for with blood money) while under the protection of my abductors; after his arrest, Dante Mamulique declared that all the suits and shoes and video games were my own property.

I went back to my normal routine: I prepare gourmet coffee in the mornings while Aunt Rosa Gloria Chagoyán, with the assistance of her aluminum walker, fetches bread; I write three movie reviews a week, occasionally go to the bank, the Treasury, or the property registry; I stream new and old movies at all hours of the day, do my weekly cinematic marathons in multiplexes on the other side of the border. I'm considered a citizen activist who helped capture a public enemy, so my laser visa is respected at any checkpoint.

On the internet I read that Jacobo Montaña had been extradited. He's doing life in a federal prison in the United States. I don't know how heavily that weighs on him: even during the days in the bunker, he seemed like a dethroned emperor.

I remembered something that Jacobo perhaps misses in his new abode: the plastic garden of his underground home, with its scent of gardenias and Arabian jasmine. I wish I had a souvenir—a plant pot would be enough—of that artificial illusion, and I'm sure he does too. I remembered something he said during our final interview:

I'm going to tell you that story because I love you but don't know you. Did Jacobo Montaña ever love or know me? Did I ever love or know him, even if only as a fictional character? That is another of the many questions for which I have no answer. A good story should be a question, not an answer. After all, as the most cynical of my university lecturers—he taught marketing and creativity—used to say: "Don't fool yourself: that thing you call 'human experience' is just a massacre of onion layers."

JULIÁN HERBERT was born in Acapulco in 1971. He is a writer, musician, and teacher, and is the author of *The House of the Pain of Others* and *Tomb Song,* as well as several volumes of poetry and two short-story collections. He is the singer in the rock band Los Tigres de Borges and lives in Saltillo, Mexico.

CHRISTINA MACSWEENEY is the translator of *The House of the Pain of Others* and *Tomb Song* by Julián Herbert. She was awarded the 2016 Valle Inclán Translation Prize for her translation of Valeria Luiselli's *The Story of My Teeth,* and her translation of Daniel Saldaña París's novel *Among Strange Victims* was shortlisted for the 2017 Best Translated Book Award. She has also published translations, articles, and interviews on a wide variety of platforms, and contributed to the anthologies *Bogotá39: New Voices from Latin America*; *México20: New Voices, Old Traditions*; *Lunatics, Lovers and Poets: Twelve Stories after Cervantes and Shakespeare*; and *Crude Words: Contemporary Writing from Venezuela.*

The text of *Bring Me the Head of Quentin Tarantino*
is set in Warnock Pro. Book design by Rachel Holscher.
Composition by Bookmobile Design and Digital
Publisher Services, Minneapolis, Minnesota.
Manufactured by Versa Press on acid-free,
30 percent postconsumer wastepaper.